THE ORB OF CAIRADO

signed by the author

KATHERINE ADDISON

Published by Solaris Books
2026

THE ORB OF CAIRADO

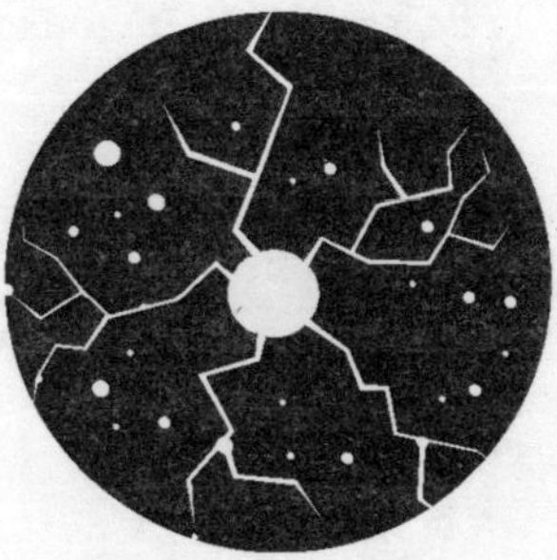

Also by Katherine Addison

The Goblin Emperor
The Witness for the Dead
The Grief of Stones
The Tomb of Dragons

The Angel of the Crows

THE ORB OF CAIRADO

KATHERINE ADDISON

SOLARIS

First published 2026 by Solaris
an imprint of Rebellion Publishing Ltd,
Riverside House, Osney Mead,
Oxford, OX2 0ES, UK

www.solarisbooks.com

ISBN: 978-1-83786-649-6

10 9 8 7 6 5 4 3 2 1

A CIP catalogue record for this book is available from the British Library.

Designed & typeset by Rebellion Publishing

Printed in the UK

1

When the *Wisdom of Choharo* crashed (he would figure out later), Ulcetha Zhorvena was halfway out Neliän Mulabin's window, praying that the fire escape was sturdier than it looked.

"Zhorvena, your *glasses,*" Osmin Mulabin hissed, holding them out to him, and shouted over her shoulder, "Just a *minute,* Father!"

"Ah, gods, thank you." He crammed them on his face and half-fell the rest of the way onto the fire escape rails. Which hurt.

"Bruises tomorrow," he muttered, but he was already on his way down, even as she slammed the window shut. He could imagine her pulling herself up and putting on her frostiest expression before going to open the door to her choleric and suspicious father. She had told Ulcetha once that she had been fighting with her father since she was sixteen, and that was at least fifteen years' practice right there.

He dropped from the bottom of the fire escape, landing safely on the balls of his feet. It was pitch-black in the alley, with only a faint nimbus from the nearest gaslight on the street to help guide him out from between the buildings. He managed well enough, though, and made no noise loud enough that Osmer Mulabar would hear it.

He walked home cheerfully through Cairado's midnight bustle, for it was truly a city that did not sleep. The municipal ferries weren't running, but there were goblin ferries (so-called, even though half the ferrymen were elves), and he picked one mostly at random for the trip across the Athamara.

His teenage goblin ferryman sang snatches of opera all the way across. Ulcetha dug out most of the spare change in his pockets to pay him when they reached the other side, and they wished each other a good night. From there, he walked through the cramped and twisted streets of East Shore to the converted palace where he had a one-room apartment with a glorious view of the river and went to bed. He slept well.

And all the time, Mara was dead. Burned and mangled and dead in the worst airship crash that had ever happened.

LIKE MANY GOBLINS in Cairado, Onaba Salathgarad—tall, black-skinned, eyes of a brooding firelight red—ran an import-export business. Ulcetha sometimes wondered morbidly whether the others were honest, or if they were all as crooked as his employer, who also did a brisk business in fake artifacts. He had no prejudices: he sold fake elven artifacts to the Barizheisei just as happily as he sold fake Barizheise artifacts to the elves—

and he sold both kinds over the mountains and across the sea. Nothing was sacred in Salathgarad's shop.

Ulcetha hated him.

Salathgarad sneered at Ulcetha's education, but exploited him as ruthlessly as he exploited his other assets; one of Ulcetha's main tasks was writing fake provenances for the fake elven artifacts that came into Salathgarad's hands. (He knew nothing whatsoever about Salathgarad's sources, and Salathgarad watched jealously to be sure that did not change.) It was a terrible use of second-class honors in history, but Ulcetha gritted his teeth and did it anyway because he was paid extremely well. He even came to find the work perversely interesting. His own specialty being narrowly the reign of Edrevenivar the Conqueror and its effects on the cities of the south, he perforce learned a great deal about relations between Cairado and the great city Vasthorno at diverse periods; about the reigns of Prince Coluna and Prince Lizhana; about the doomed princess Hathiän; and about the work of the great jeweler, Dachensol Tobora Theramar.

It was work, he reminded himself daily. Crooked work, but work all the same, and without it he would be living in a tenement instead of a converted palace or even facing the municipal House of Indigents where his shame would be complete. So he kept his hatred for Salathgarad behind his teeth, kept his head down, and kept his job.

In writing fake provenances, Ulcetha also learned a great deal about the history of the lost treasures of Cairado, not because Salathgarad was stupid enough to fake them, but because so many of his Ethuverazheise fakes ended up being somehow tangential to them.

The Orb of Cairado was a flawless star sapphire as large as an egg. It had been presented to Prince Olnera by the man who found it some seventeen hundred years ago and made promptly into a scepter to symbolize the princes of Cairado. It had remained in Cairado until it was given—or "given"—to the prince of Vasthorno in exchange for Cairado's independence from the larger and much more powerful city. The princes and people of Cairado had lamented this loss for two hundred years before the Orb returned to the city as part of the dowry of Hathiän Estervin.

Hathiän's dowry also included the Star of Cstheio, a blue diamond the size of a man's thumbnail. Some long-ago prince of Vasthorno had had it set into a ring for his wife, and it had since passed from mother-in-law to daughter-in-law in an unbroken chain. Sending it to Cairado was a measure of how desperate Hathiän's father was to see her married before her "nervousness" devolved irredeemably into madness, which all parties involved knew it was going to. Ulcetha had come to have no good opinion of Prince Shevora, who had married Hathiän anyway for the sake of her dowry.

Hathiän died insane when her son was an infant, and the Star of Cstheio remained simply a treasure of the princes of Cairado… until it became urgently necessary in the wake of Orava the Usurper, the only maza ever to attempt to use his powers to take the throne, to prove the good will and loyalty of the Cairad'athmaz'are before the people of Cairado stormed the Cairad'mazan'theileian and killed every maza they could find. The prince and the Cairad'athmaza had cobbled together a ceremony involving the Orb of Cairado and the Star of Cstheio, which was then repeated yearly until the coming of Edrevenivar the Conqueror.

This bit, Ulcetha had already known. Prince Rinava, whose son had been killed in the futile defense of Vasthorno, had put all of the treasures of the Moraclada in a vault deep beneath the

Summer Palace of Cleth and then—when Edrevenivar's armies were busy razing Vasthorno to the ground—burned down the palace with himself inside. And Corica Athmaza had hidden the Star of Cstheio and then gone mad, coming to believe that everyone around him was an agent of Edrevenivar; all he would ever say about the Star was that it was hidden where Edrevenivar would never find it. And that part was true.

WHEN PEOPLE WERE asking each other later, Ulcetha knew exactly where he'd been when he learned about the crash of the *Wisdom of Choharo*. He'd been in Salathgarad's small but elegant office, struggling to make the public books and the private books balance in a way that looked innocent on one side and was accurate on the other.

Salathgarad banged through the door as he always did, but instead of yelling, he stood quietly until Ulcetha and Eda were both looking at him in puzzlement and said, "They're saying the emperor's airship crashed."

"Crashed?" said Eda.

"Do you know which airship it was?" said Ulcetha.

Salathgarad said, "Does it matter?"

"Yes," Ulcetha said, much closer to snapping at Salathgarad than was probably wise. "It matters to me."

"The *Wisdom of Choharo*," Salathgarad said instead of snapping back, and Ulcetha put his head in his hands, cold with horror. Mara was the pilot on that ship.

Eda said, "Is the emperor…"

"Dead," Salathgarad said bleakly. "He and his sons."

And the airship crew, Ulcetha added, but even if he'd been willing to chance Salathgarad's temper a second time, he couldn't get the words out.

Salathgarad said abruptly, "I'm closing the office for the day. You two go home."

Neither Ulcetha nor Eda waited for Salathgarad to change his mind.

MARA AND ULCETHA had been friends since earliest childhood, and they had stayed friends even when their lives went in radically different directions. Mara was the only person who had attended Ulcetha's second-class honors ceremony; none of his family could be bothered. Mara had also stayed by him when he was asked to leave the University of Cairado, another thing his family couldn't be bothered to do, and Ulcetha had sworn to himself that he would do as much for Mara, should the opportunity—gods forbid—arise. And now neither that nor any other opportunity would ever present itself.

Ulcetha was confident that Mara had died knowing that Ulcetha was his friend and that he loved him, but the balance between them was out of true. He thought there was nothing that could fix it, that this was just one more place in his life where things were off-kilter, his entire life out of whack, but that was before Sinzharo showed up at his door.

Sinzharo was Mara's wife—widow now. She and Ulcetha had hated each other on sight and had both tried to hide it for Mara's sake. Ulcetha sometimes suspected they hadn't done a very good job, but if Mara knew, he said nothing. Mara would do anything to avoid a fight; pretending not to see what they were trying to hide was no more than the flick of an ear.

Ulcetha had fully expected never to see Sinzharo again, and his face and ears must have shown as much when he opened the door, for she sounded both nervous and apologetic when she said, “Hello Ulcetha.”

“Hello, Sinzharo,” he said, and by rote, “I am sorry for your loss.” Then he looked at her more carefully and felt much less rote about it.

No one had been sleeping well in the week since news of the crash had reached Cairado, between grief—whether personal or part of the strange public grief for someone you had never met, never expected to meet, and maybe hadn’t liked—and nervousness edging up on fear about what the new emperor (Edrehasivar, he was calling himself, and what did *that* mean?) might choose to do in the wake of his father and brothers’ deaths, but Sinzharo behind her careful maquillage looked as if she hadn’t slept at *all*.

“Thank you,” she said. “Would you… would you come have a drink with me? I have something I need to talk to you about.”

“To *me*? That is, yes, of course. Just let me get my shoes.”

They walked in silence a block and a half to the Cat and Carpenter, where they found a table and each ordered a glass of the house Romaki. They sat, still in silence—for what in the world was there to say to each other?—until the wine came.

Sinzharo took a swallow of wine as if fortifying herself and said, “I found something in Mara’s desk that had your name on it.”

Ulcetha was surprised she’d brought it to him, but had the wit not to say so. He waited, taking a sip of wine himself, and Sinzharo pulled a long envelope from her inside jacket pocket. He saw that she’d opened it, but didn’t say anything about that, either. Instead, he took out the piece of paper inside and unfolded it to reveal…

"A map?" he said, looking at Sinzharo.

Her bafflement was plain in her ears; she said, "He never talked about wanting to go to the Vershaleen Islands to me. Did he to you?"

"No," Ulcetha said. He took his glasses off and examined the map more closely. "This isn't a standard map. You can see where it was torn out of a book."

"Yes," said Sinzharo. "But I have no idea which book it might be, nor if that's important."

"You think it must be something important?"

"Mara went to some trouble to be sure you got it," she said. "He wouldn't have done that on a whim."

"No, but there's nothing marked on the map."

"I know," Sinzharo said. "It's just a map of the Vershaleen Islands, and I have no idea why he wanted you to have it."

"There wasn't anything else with it?" Ulcetha checked the envelope again.

"No," said Sinzharo, either missing or not resenting the implication that she might have interfered with the envelope's contents.

They both drank more wine.

"Do you think the map came out of a book Mara owned?"

"He wouldn't have torn a map out of a book he'd borrowed. Frankly, I'm surprised he tore a map out of a book at all."

"It does seem unlike him. Which suggests that, as you said, this is something that was important to him."

"Yes," said Sinzharo. "The Witness for the Dead tried, but he couldn't get anything from Mara's body. So I just… I'm trying to do what I think Mara would want."

"Yes," Ulcetha said. No matter how much he disliked her, he

had never doubted that Sinzharo loved Mara. "Clearly, you're right. He wanted me to have this map. I just wish I had any idea why."

Sinzharo shook her head, making the black beads of her earrings clatter together. "I don't know, but if I think of something, I promise I'll tell you."

"Thank you," Ulcetha said, and they finished the wine in a silence that was almost companionable.

2

Despite Sinzharo's promise, Ulcetha thought it unlikely that anything more would come of Mara's inexplicable bequest. Mara had been intensely private—he had loved secrets and mysteries and puzzles—and he had liked to keep the various pieces of his life quite separate from one another. So it seemed most probable that this was some piece of Mara's life that he had never gotten around to telling Ulcetha about.

But two days later, Sinzharo was on his doorstep again. She said, "I thought of something," without bothering with a greeting.

"Hello, Sinzharo," Ulcetha said. "What did you think of?"

"What if it isn't the *map* you're supposed to have at all? What if it's the book?"

"The book the map is from, you mean?"

"Yes! He couldn't put the book in an envelope that would fit in his desk, so he tore the map out."

"Why not just write the name of the book on a piece of paper?" Ulcetha objected.

"I don't know. But you know how secretive Mara was. Perhaps he wanted to be sure that nobody going through his things would know what the map was for." She again seemed unresentful of the implication that Mara had suspected her of prying.

"Well, he succeeded in that," said Ulcetha.

"But we agreed it must have come from a book he owned. Do you want to come look at them? There aren't very many."

Ulcetha found himself unexpectedly touched by Sinzharo's restraint: she could easily have looked through the books by herself. It wouldn't have taken her long to figure out which of them, if any, was missing a map.

"Let me get my shoes," he said.

Mara and Sinzharo had lived, and Sinzharo still did live, in a five-room flat on Bruncavar Avenue, four blocks from Ulcetha's palace apartment. Although Mara and Ulcetha's habit had been to meet at the Roan Mare in Ribbons, Ulcetha had been here once or twice; he remembered the bookshelves along one wall of the long front room, which held vases of flowers and a variety of trinkets Mara had brought back from his travels, but also a surprising number of books for an unscholarly household. Most of them were books Sinzharo had inherited from her father, who had been a literary scholar at the University, but there had been a few that Mara had picked up here and there. Most of those were, in fact, the sort of books that would have maps in them, and for a moment Ulcetha thought he was going to have to sit on the floor and go through each of them looking for torn edges. But comparison with the map showed that three books were too large and five books were too small, and that left only a thin book bound in blue leather; the title was in Pencharnin, but he recognized the word *Chadevan*. He slid the book out of the bookcase, and when he opened it, it flopped open to the middle, where something had clearly been torn out. He put the book down on the end table and got out the map again The map was the right size, the paper was the right color, and when he tried, the ragged edge of the map lined up perfectly with the ragged edge of paper left in the book.

"I don't know that that gets us much farther," he said to Sinzharo.

"He wanted you to have that book," Sinzharo said.

"Yes, but *why?*"

"Mara could have answered that," she said. "I can't. In any event, you are welcome to the book, and I am glad to have the riddle solved."

But the riddle isn't *solved,* Ulcetha protested, but only to himself. He thanked Sinzharo for the book and walked home again.

He took his shoes off at the door and then sat cross-legged on the divan that served as his bed—and seating for guests, if he had ever had any guests—and contemplated the Pencharnin book.

He and Mara had never discussed the Chadevan Sea that he could recall. He had not known Mara owned this book. As far as he knew, Mara had not been able to read Pencharnin, and he was fairly confident he would have known. So what in the name of all that was holy...

He flipped through the book, noting illustrations and several other maps, and guessed it had to be a travelers' guide of some sort. Not that that helped him. He looked at the pages on either side of the torn-out map, but aside from the word "Vershaleen," he saw nothing that he recognized. "This is ridiculous, Mara," he said aloud.

He looked at the flyleaf, where Mara's name was neatly written. He looked at the endpapers: nothing except, at the back, a printed list that he thought had to be other books in this series of travelers' guides. Finally, in desperation (and because in truth he had nothing better to do until seven o'clock, when he was meeting Osmin Delbrathin for dinner), he began paging through, looking for marks or marginalia or *anything* that might offer a hint as to why Mara had so cryptically pointed him at this book.

He found it three pages after the torn-out map. He didn't even recognize it at first, seeing it so radically out of context, but after several moments of staring blankly at the random-looking combination of letters and numbers, he realized it was an index number for the Library Harcenada, the Harceneise.

And then he stared at it in, if possible, even blanker bewilderment. What could Mara have possibly had to do with the Harceneise? Why had he written an index number in this Pencharneise travelers' guide and gone to such peculiar lengths to lead Ulcetha to it?

"Oh, Mara," he said, torn between frustration and laughter, and feeling hollowed out with grief, "what *is* this?" It was exactly the sort of thing that happened in the adventure novels both of them guiltily loved. And Mara liked complicated things, like pocket-watches. So Ulcetha could imagine Mara setting up a paper chase like this just because he could, for the sheer joy of doing it. It was in fact the only explanation that made sense.

After a while he organized himself. There were two lines of questioning here. First, what was the index number pointing to? Second, why had Mara written it in this book? The second, he thought, might be more answerable when he knew the answer to the first, which helpfully prioritized them. But finding the answer to the first was going to be more than slightly tricky.

Once upon a time, as a scholar second-class of the University of Cairado, Ulcetha had been in the Harceneise almost daily, and he knew the key to the index numbers. The first three letters told you which of the Library's five towers the book was in, the first number was the floor of the tower, the second set of letters the bookcase, the second number the shelf, and the third number in parenthesis was where the book came in the sequence of books on the shelf. It was a remarkably efficient system and it worked, he knew, almost all the time. But a book misplaced might never be found again. Allegedly, it never happened—the Library's small army of shelvers were rigorously trained—but Ulcetha knew better than to believe that.

And how easy, he thought, to hide a book! Put it on the wrong shelf in the wrong tower, and no one but you would ever know where it was. And if you wrote down the *actual* location, as for instance in a Pencharneise travelers' guide, you could retrieve it whenever you wanted to. If, of course, you had borrowing privileges at the Library, which Ulcetha no longer did and Mara never had.

Over the next week, as it became steadily less likely that Edrehasivar VII would start his reign with a purge, Ulcetha thought about that index number on and off. He had never been able to resist a puzzle—which Mara, an inveterate lover of puzzles, had known perfectly well—and he was deeply frustrated, once again, that his deal with Sevara only got him into the Harceneise once a week, and then only into the Reading Room.

Sevara was a captain of shelvers. It had been common knowledge in the Department that Sevara was amenable to making "special arrangements" with anyone who could pay generously enough, so it had not been difficult, when Ulcetha started working for Salathgarad, to come to an agreement.

Once a week, Sevara left the outside door to the Reading Room unlocked, giving Ulcetha access to the card catalogues, and every week he left a neat stack of the books Ulcetha had requested the week before. He did *not* unlock the door to the stacks, and nothing would induce him to. Ulcetha knew because he'd tried.

Ulcetha could simply add Mara's index number to his list for the week, but without knowing exactly what was waiting at PLU 3 AP 2 (49) he was loath to do so. It would be *very* like Mara to have put something there that wasn't a book at all. He needed to get into the stacks, and there was no way to do that that would not bring him face-to-face with a shelver or a librarian, and most likely sooner rather than later.

Unless he broke in at night.

This was a foolish idea, and he tried to scoff at it, but it kept recurring. There were windows on the ground floor that were big enough to climb through; they were kept locked, but the more he thought about it, the more he thought he was willing to break a window to solve this puzzle.

He would need a light, but that was easy enough. He had a small adjustable lantern that only needed to be washed and filled. He did that while arguing with himself that this was a stupid thing even to be *contemplating*; if he was caught, he would probably be thrown in the river (that being a far simpler way of dealing with criminals than putting them in prison—and if he was put in prison, he would almost certainly die of one of the pestilential fevers that haunted the Goremet before his case even went before a judiciar), and everyone who had known him at the University would say, "See, there? Once a thief, always a thief."

And yet he could not leave the puzzle alone.

He found an old black and plum scarf to cover his hair. His mourning coat was shabby, but certainly black enough for these purposes. He knew that real thieves—those with enough elven blood to be pale skinned—used grease or mud or soot to darken their faces and hands, but he wasn't quite sure when he was supposed to do that (before he left his apartment? thereby demonstrating to everyone who saw him on the streets that he intended to do something illegal?) and in the end decided not to.

He was in fact still arguing with himself about whether he was going to do this insane thing at all when, at midnight, he put on the mourning coat, put the black and plum scarf in his pocket, and carefully locked his apartment door behind him as he left. *Ulcetha, this is madness!* But he was doing it anyway.

He took a goblin ferry across the Athamara and walked to the Harceneise, looming great and black against the blackness of the sky. Sevara had shown him the trick of getting over the wall, that one loose brick that could be removed to make a perfect step, and once on the inside, he tied the scarf over his hair and adjusted his lantern from *late-night stroll* to *wrong-doing,* then carefully skirted the building to the base of the northeast tower and the lowest bank of windows.

He was not quite sure about how to break a window without telling everyone in earshot that someone was committing a crime at the Harceneise, and while he was thinking about it, he tried the windows. The fifth along wasn't locked.

He shoved it all the way open, stood on tiptoe to set his lantern on the floor, and then heaved himself, not gracefully, over the windowsill. He kept from cursing aloud even as he half-fell into the building, then picked himself up, put the scarf back on his head, and, leaving the window open in case of a hasty exit, he opened the lantern an inch wider and began to look for the stairs.

The Harceneise was unsettling at night, although he wondered if he'd mind as much if he hadn't just struggled in illicitly through a window. Even the rows of full bookcases—and a full bookcase was normally the friendliest object Ulcetha could imagine—looked distressingly unlike themselves in the lantern-light, as if they might at any moment prove to be haunted. He was glad to find the stairs, although there the darkness was even heavier.

He climbed to the third floor and there found his way from Bookcase AA to Bookcase AP. Second shelf counting from the top, and then across from 1 to 49… where there was a stout volume on the customs of the Neschonori region of Barizhan, index number properly pasted on its spine and all. He picked it up and opened it and nearly dropped it in shock.

Someone had taken this book on the Neschonori and hollowed it out, gluing the outer edges of all the pages together to form a box. And in the box was an object that Ulcetha immediately recognized, since he had been accused of stealing it five years ago and had never been able to prove his innocence.

It was called the Orish Veltavan. It had been discovered only five and a half years ago, by Osmer Bruna Aidrina, a scholar first-class of the University of Cairado, who spent most of his time in the Cleth Valley, excavating the Summer Palace and searching for the treasure hidden beneath it. People had laughed at Osmer Aidrina for years for pursuing this wonder-tale treasure until he came back with the Orish Veltavan, which everyone had frankly thought was a myth.

The only problem was, although the stories agreed that the Orish Veltavan was the key to finding the Orb of Cairado, none of them said *how*. It had been the secret of the direct line of the House Moraclada and had died with Prince Rinava. And the object itself had not proved informative. Debate in the Department of History had been sharp and creative… until the Orish Veltavan disappeared.

Osmer Aidrina had aged twenty years overnight.

The entire Department had searched frantically, and the clearer it became that the Orish Veltavan was nowhere to be found, the more Ulcetha, who was at that time the custodian of the Department's small and valuable collection of artifacts, came under suspicion, until finally, the Orish Veltavan apparently gone for good, Osmer Harcenar, the head of the Department, said he thought everyone would be happier if Ulcetha left.

Ulcetha had protested—for one, he hadn't taken it, for another, if he had, wouldn't it be better to try to make him give it back?—but Osmer Harcenar would not listen. Within a week, the entire city knew that Ulcetha Zhorvena had been thrown out of the University for stealing, and everyone he knew—except for Mara—stopped talking to him.

Had Mara known where it was the entire time? Was that why he alone had said, "I'm sure you didn't do it"?

But Mara couldn't have stolen it. The one thing that had been absolutely clear after all the searching was that the Orish Veltavan must have been taken by someone with a Department key, meaning a scholar third-class or above. Not Mara Lilana, who had never set foot on the University campus more than twice in his life.

None of it made any sense, and Ulcetha did not know what to do.

If he left the Orish Veltavan here and did nothing... no, that was the worst option, since it meant the Orish Veltavan stayed lost. If he took it and was caught with it—well, they already thought he was a thief. If he took it and went to... whom? Not Osmer Harcenar, who would never believe he was *not* a thief. He couldn't take it to Osmer Aidrina because Osmer Aidrina had gone down into the Below-palace four years ago and never come back up. He flipped through a mental roster of scholars first-class: Osmer Elivera, Osmer Melorar, Osmer Ledmenar, Osmer Trenevar… Osmer Trenevar. He doubted any of the scholars first-class would listen to him if he tried to just show up in their workroom and say, "I found the Orish Veltavan hidden in the Harceneise." But Osmer Trenevar *might*. Osmer Trenevar wanted to find the Orb of Cairado almost as much as Osmer Aidrina had. And with Osmer Trenevar, he had another avenue of approach to try. With Osmer Trenevar, he had Csecoro.

3

After his banishment from the Department of History, desperate for scholarly conversation, Ulcetha had gone to the salon of Dach'osmin Bruncavin, half convinced they would turn him away, too. But they let him in. The salon, held weekly in the ballroom of the Bruncavada compound, welcomed female scholars in all disciplines: historians, mathematicians, astronomers, literary scholars, philosophers. Osmin Vishnevin was a maza—a mazo, properly, but she said she did not like the word. The scholars were elves of all ages, from barely sixteen to well over ninety, and even if they were not all friends, none of them were enemies.

He was not the only man there. There were others who sympathized with the women's ambitions and attended the salons to show support (the elderly Dach'osmer Bruncavar among them). Osmin Thorobin had even married one of them, becoming Osmerrem Ponevaran and the only married woman in regular attendance. "There are always women who try to do both," Dach'osmin Bruncavin said sadly, "but so many men oppose learning for women that it is rare to find a husband who will permit his wife even to come here, much less to pursue her own studies."

"And a woman in charge of a household, with children and servants and husband—and social duties, paying visits, being paid visits—so rarely has the *time*," said Osmin Narlezin.

"Time is the first thing one loses," said Osmerrem Levornaran, a childless widow who had been welcomed back to the salon on her husband's death. (From all Ulcetha could gather, Osmer Levornar was not much mourned, and for good reason.) "There's always something more important than one's own pursuits. *Always*."

Ulcetha thought, but was not about to say, that if they thought being a married noblewoman was difficult, they should try being a shopkeeper's wife, with all the same demands and only half the budget and only a maid-of-all-work to help. He was scared enough of betraying his bourgeois origin; he wasn't going to confess to it.

Ulcetha assumed they knew of his disgrace—assumed, when he thought it over later, that that was exactly *why* they let him in, as another way to defy the men of the Department of History—but none of them was rude enough to say so, and the historians in particular welcomed him gladly. The coming of Edrevenivar was one of Cairado's collective preoccupations, and three of the women were doing research that dovetailed with Ulcetha's own. He had many fascinating conversations with Osmin Garmozhin, who had been studying the destruction of Vasthorno for forty years, and made Ulcetha's own thesis on the subject look like a nursery rhyme. And Osmin Crelcorin was endlessly interested in the careers of Edrevenivar's generals; she explained Edrevenivar's southern campaigns far more clearly than Osmer Melorar had, and Ulcetha began to have at least a dim understanding of why some people specialized in military history.

And then—after he'd been there long enough, or said enough of the right things, he still didn't know—they started inviting him to research in their family archives. This was a coup that would have had Ulcetha's former friends drooling with envy. Access to family archives was a privilege the scholars first-class tended to keep for themselves, and the salon members went to considerable trouble to give Ulcetha access without letting their fathers and brothers know. Neliän Mulabin's was not the only window he had gone out of to escape detection. The women seemed to find it more amusement than nuisance, and Ulcetha could no more have turned down what they were offering than a starving man could have turned down a banquet.

He could not even say now how his relationship with Csecoro had transformed from research to intimacy, except that he was quite sure that it had been her idea to take things into the bedroom. He would never have had the nerve—courage or effrontery, depending on one's point of view—to proposition Osmer Trenevar's sister, although he could also admit that he hadn't had the nobility of spirit to say no when she made the suggestion.

Despite the fact that he made more money as Salathgarad's clerk than he had as a scholar second-class of the University, his life was not a happy one, but Csecoro was a good fraction of what made it bearable. He did not make the mistake of imagining it was anything serious to her—he was just trying to make it last as long as possible.

ULCETHA WAITED UNTIL after they had had sex to broach the matter.

Csecoro was lying naked across the bed, grinning up at the ceiling, her milk-white hair hanging in a great half unraveled braid over the side to the floor. Ulcetha, who was mostly responsible for the state of her hair, sat beside her and began working out the plaited knots and tangles. He said, "Wouldst do something for me?"

She turned her head to look at him upside down. Like most noble elven families in Cairado, the Trenevada had a hint of Barizheise blood several ancestors back in their family tree. In Csecoro, this manifested as a haze of gold in her large, pale gray eyes, making them almost opalescent and quite beautiful. "Anything," she said. "What needest thou?"

"I need to talk to thy brother."

"To Vora? Whatever for?"

Ulcetha winced but said carefully, "It is probably better if I don't tell thee."

"Ulcetha! What trouble hast thou found now?"

"It's not trouble," he said. "It might be the opposite of trouble. But Osmer Trenevar will quite rightfully be angry with me if I talk about it outside the Department."

"Oh, the *Department,*" said Csecoro. "May all the gods forfend we do anything to upset the *Department*." Csecoro would have been a scholar first-class by now if the University would have let her in.

"I'm sorry," Ulcetha said.

"It isn't *thy* fault. And, yes, I will gladly speak to Vora for thee. Thou wishest to speak with him. When and where?"

"Noon tomorrow at the sundial in the Gardens Melorinada."

"Like something out of a novel," Csecoro said, amused.

"I know," Ulcetha said. "But it's the best I can do. Tomorrow's my day off, and I know of no better place."

THE GARDENS MELORINADA, which extended along both sides of the Athamara just outside the Third Wall, were lush with rhododendrons and azaleas and ordennas. They were laid out in spirals and knots and not-quite-mazes, and were an assignation point for all kinds of meetings; it was considered good manners to ignore anyone you encountered in the gardens who was not your assignee. Ulcetha, having ignored two women and an anxious-looking man, reached the sundial in its circle of palest pink azaleas a good twenty minutes early, and so had plenty of time to sit on a bench and rehearse what he was going to say.

Several people ignored him as they went by and he ignored them in turn.

The sundial, a great mosaic circle with a six-foot gnomon, was showing five minutes past noon when Osmer Vora Trenevar arrived.

Osmer Trenevar looked eerily like his sister, although they were not twins. The same cheekbones, the same arching eyebrows, and the same gray-gold eyes. The red first-class ribbons in his braids had been ironed that morning and stood out beautifully against his blue and gold brocade coat.

Ulcetha stood up nervously at his approach.

"Mer Zhorvena," said Osmer Trenevar with a polite inclination of his head.

"Osmer Trenevar," Ulcetha said. "Thank you for—"

"Yes, yes. We can skip that part. What did you want to talk to me about?"

Ulcetha hesitated; then, forgetting all his carefully rehearsed, subtle lines, he blurted, "I found the Orish Veltavan."

Osmer Trenevar stared at him in blank disbelief. "You… *found* the Orish Veltavan?"

"It was hidden in the Harceneise," Ulcetha said. "I only found it because a… a friend who died in the wreck of the *Wisdom of Choharo* left me a clue."

"*What?*"

Ulcetha explained as best he could, although he was afraid that more words did not make what had happened make more sense. "I don't have any idea how Mara got the index number or how he knew what it was." *Or why he didn't bring it to me straight away,* but that was a question for midnight insomnia, not for a discussion with Osmer Trenevar.

Who looked like he'd been hit in the face with something heavy. "Do you… do you have it with you?"

He did, because he hadn't been able to think of any other way to prove that he was telling the truth. He took it out of his pocket, unwrapped the black and plum scarf, and said, "Here. I really did find it."

Osmer Trenevar looked at the Orish Veltavan carefully, without touching it. It was a strange looking object, a swirl of hardened gold wire strung with jewel chips. Osmer Aidrina had been convinced the positioning of the jewels was somehow important and had taken careful notes and measurements trying to figure out the directions and distances between them. Others had theorized there was a locked door somewhere in the Below-palace and the Orish Veltavan was a literal key. Ulcetha had tried but had been unable to imagine a lock with pin tumblers so eccentric that the Orish Veltavan would activate them. Everybody had had a theory, and it had looked like Osmer Aidrina would for once have no difficulty in staffing his expedition. But then the Orish Veltavan disappeared.

"And you've brought it," Osmer Trenevar said, "to me. Why?"

"For help," Ulcetha said. "I know how insane my story sounds. But if you vouched for me, I think even Osmer Harcenar would believe me."

"Ah. And what do I get in return?"

"I..." Ulcetha had been prepared, more or less, for *why should I believe you?* But this question had not occurred to him. "What do you want?"

Osmer Trenevar smiled. "I want to find the Orb of Cairado before anyone else does."

"All right," Ulcetha said, "but I don't see how—"

"I'm sure poor Aidrina was right," said Osmer Trenevar. "This is a map. All we have to do is figure out how to follow it."

"You make that sound easy," Ulcetha said, "but—"

"Have you ever been to the Cleth Valley?"

"No," Ulcetha said. Given his preference, he did not leave the city.

"That's a shame," said Osmer Trenevar. "Because it's much easier to envision if you've *seen* the descent to the Below-palace. But I agree with Aidrina that this"—and he gestured along a length of wire that could have been the top or the bottom—"is that descent, and the first jewel here is what they call the Antechamber. And I think if you and I go out there with the Orish Veltavan, we'll find other rooms of the caves that line up with the jewels."

"Both of us? But you don't need me along for that," Ulcetha said.

"I'm not as foolish as Aidrina. I have no intention of going down there alone. And this is what I want. If you go with me and help me find the Orb of Cairado, I will vouch for you to Harcenar and the University Senate. You may take it or"—Osmer Trenevar shrugged fine-boned shoulders—"leave it."

Ulcetha tried to think about Osmer Trenevar's deal rationally, but there wasn't really much to think about. "All right," he said. "I'll do it."

"Good," said Trenevar. "How soon can you be ready to leave?"

"*Leave?* But don't we need… I don't know, equipment? Osmer Aidrina always—"

"Aidrina had his own way of doing things," Trenevar said dismissively. "I'll take care of supplies. If you can pack lightly, we won't need more than one pack horse."

Ulcetha tried to adjust his definition of "packing lightly" down to what Trenevar seemed to mean. "All right," he said, although he knew his ears reflected his dubiousness.

"Can you be ready to leave tomorrow?"

"*Tomorrow?*"

"I'm not teaching this quarter and have no reason to wait. Do you?"

Ulcetha thought about Salathgarad and his probable reaction to anyone asking for a week off. He thought with a sudden sensation of lightness that if this worked, and they found the Orb of Cairado, he would never have to see Salathgarad or that elegant office again. "No," he said. "I suppose not."

"Excellent. Then let's meet at Princess Paviän's Gate at… seven?"

Ulcetha was supposed to be at work at seven-thirty. "All right," he said and hoped he would not regret it.

4

Princess Paviän's Gate was the main gate in the Second Wall of the city, beautifully set with ceramic tiles. There was, Ulcetha knew from Csecoro, whose research specialty was the reign of Princess Paviän's husband Prince Armetha, an entire small industry of ceramicists—supported mainly by the municipal government—devoted to maintaining those tiles and replacing them as inevitably needed. He was not in a mood to appreciate it, having just tacked his notice to Salathgarad's door and well and truly burned his bridges, but the gate was exquisite in the early morning sun, its azure and scarlet traceries contrasting vividly against the white tiles.

He found Trenevar, who was standing at the north side of the gate next to a hitching post, and three horses, two saddled and one carrying whatever supplies Trenevar had deemed necessary. He was wearing an ostentatiously plain green coat with green cloth buttons. Ulcetha, who had ended up wearing his mourning coat, as being the plainest he had and also the one he would regret least if it was torn or otherwise damaged, felt a little less ridiculous.

"Oh, good, Zhorvena. Good morning," said Trenevar. "Is that valise all you have?"

"Yes," Ulcetha said. It had taken considerable effort to pare his necessities down to what would fit in one valise, but he had done it. Trenevar took the valise and secured it behind the saddle of the dun horse.

"I assume," Trenevar said, trying to make it sound like a joke but obviously deadly serious, "that you remembered the Orish Veltavan?"

"I did," said Ulcetha. He patted his coat lightly over the inner pocket. "I have it safe."

'Good," Trenevar said; his smile made him look even more disconcertingly like Csecoro. "Then I think we're ready to go."

Happily, there was a mounting block beside the post, and happily the dun horse was willing to stand at it while Ulcetha hauled himself awkwardly into the saddle.

"Not a horseman?" Trenevar said, this time sounding genuinely amused.

"Not very much," said Ulcetha.

"Well, Patraca is very placid and will be well-content to follow Albeva, so you should not have any trouble." Trenevar mounted the chestnut horse—Albeva—easily and they moved into the flow of westward traffic out the gate.

Ulcetha had taken some riding lessons—Osmer Bevanar, his mentor, had insisted on it when Ulcetha earned his third class honors—so he was not helpless on top of a horse, but he was neither graceful nor self-assured and was burningly aware of it. He tried to remember how to sit, how to position his feet in the stirrups, how to hold the reins, a frantic cascade of half-remembered instructions, while his horse, as promised, followed Trenevar's. Ulcetha's weight-shifting caused him to stop once, in almost visible confusion, but he was happy to start again.

They made slow progress at first, having to contend with the rest of the traffic on the Great West Road, which had once led, not only to the Summer Palace at Cleth, but to the city of Vasthorno, which had once been magnificent but was razed to the ground for attempting to defy Edrevenivar. The Great West Road now led to a number of villages and artisans' cooperatives and split north and south at the Pilzhalo crossroads to run to Choharo (north) and Sevezho (south), and was still the busiest road in Cairado, if you did not count the rivers.

It took them three days to reach Obaro—three nights of sleeping on sagging mattresses in roadside hotels—and another day to make the hike up into the hills. They reached the Cleth Valley near sundown; there was nothing here any longer except the ruin of the Summer Palace. The locals considered the ruin bad luck and claimed it harbored pestilence, which all of the Department scholars said was nonsense. Osmer Aidrina had excavated the site of the Summer Palace for twenty years before he disappeared, and he had never shown the slightest sign of illness—but he had had to hire his workers from Pilzhalo. No one from Obaro would have anything to do with it.

They found Osmer Aidrina's campsite, which everyone who came to the Cleth Valley used. They watered their horses in the aqueduct that ran alongside the ruins, carrying water from the hills above Cleth down to Obaro—a project of Prince Rinava's great-great-great-grandfather. Trenevar had brought grain for the horses, and the grass was lush, since there were no sheep or cattle to graze on it. Trenevar produced a ground cloth, and he and Ulcetha sat on it and ate some of the provisions Trenevar had brought—in addition to beef jerky and dried currants, he had tins of sardines and crackers to eat them on. It was warm enough not to need a fire. Ulcetha imitated Trenevar in folding his coat up to make a pillow, and although Trenevar seemed to drop off to sleep immediately, Ulcetha lay awake for a long time, staring up at the stars and turning the Orish Veltavan over and over in his hands.

His sleep was thin and uncomfortable, and he dreamed about the Harceneise burning down.

In the morning, after a slightly odd breakfast of sardines and crackers, and after Trenevar had watered the horses, they started for the Below-palace. The hills around the Cleth Valley were riddled with caves, and there were entrances to the cave system everywhere, but the Moraclada's entrance, and the one that Trenevar thought matched up with the Orish Veltavan, was actually in the ruins of the Summer Palace. Osmer Aidrina had found it less than a month before the Orish Veltavan was stolen.

Ulcetha had seen drawings of the Summer Palace; it had been a slightly absurd five-tiered cake of a building, with colonnades on every level to catch whatever breezes there might be. When it had burned, all of those colonnades had fallen in, creating a pile of rubble and ashes the size of four city blocks and in places nearly all of those five tiers tall. The wonder, as someone had remarked at the time, was not that it took Osmer Aidrina twenty years to find the Orish Veltavan; the wonder was that he found it at all.

Ulcetha followed Trenevar carefully along one of the paths cleared by Osmer Aidrina and his workmen until they came to a set of stone stairs that plunged down into the darkness beneath the ruin.

"This is the first descent," said Trenevar. He had a coil of rope slung over his shoulder, and both he and Ulcetha were carrying lanterns tied around their waists, which they now lit. "If you look at the Orish Veltavan, you'll see that that first spiral of wire down to the diamond matches it perfectly."

Ulcetha looked at the Orish Veltavan and looked at the stairs; it was hard to translate one against the other, but he thought he saw what Trenevar (and Osmer Aidrina before him) meant. Certainly he could see nothing that disproved the idea. "All right," he said.

They descended the stairs carefully. Someone had rigged a kind of hand rail out of rope, and Ulcetha blessed them for it. The stairs were steep and uneven and polished smooth with generations of feet, and it would be all too easy to slip and break an ankle.

At the base of the stairs, Trenevar said, "This is the Antechamber."

"And you say it's the diamond," Ulcetha said.

"Yes."

The Antechamber was a small, perfectly squared room, its walls carved with lilies and hibiscus, with exits leading in three directions, all sloping down. Ulcetha held up the Orish Veltavan and tried to orient it correctly to the stairs. "Then you think the next room is the topaz?"

"Yes. Which way?"

"Left, I mean north," Ulcetha said and tried to sound more certain than he felt.

They took the left-hand exit and descended by a smooth path to another chamber, also perfectly squared. This one was carved with a pattern of hexagons.

"The ruby is next," said Trenevar.

"East," said Ulcetha, "but I'm not sure how we're going to follow it, since it goes east, then straight down, then west."

"You'll see," Trenevar said.

They went east until they came to a square hole in the floor, large enough to admit a person, although you could skirt around it and keep going east if you wanted to. There were the remains of hinges on one side, suggesting there had once been a trapdoor here. Someone had sunk an iron ring into the stone on the side opposite the hinges, and there was a rope tied to it. "Like this," Trenevar said, and climbed agilely down the rope.

Grimly, Ulcetha followed him, although he was well aware he was not agile. The climb was not as bad as it could have been, though, since it was not through empty space, but along one wall of an elegantly fluted chimney. At the bottom, Trenevar said, "Good, good. Where next? Back to the west, correct?"

He had gotten out his compass, which was about the same size as a pocket-watch. Ulcetha looked at the compass and then at the Orish Veltavan and tried to visualize the one laid over the other, with only middling success. But finally he said, "Yes. We want to go west. But what about the rope?"

"What about it?"

"Why was it there?"

"It was Aidrina's rope, but no one wanted to untie it, in case poor Aidrina found his way back to it."

"Oh," said Ulcetha and failed to prevent himself imagining

the horror of finding your way back through the dark to the place a rope was supposed to be, and no rope being there.

"Come on," Trenevar said impatiently.

And since the last thing Ulcetha wanted was to be left alone down here in the dark, he followed Trenevar.

THEY TRACED THE path of the Orish Veltavan, jewel by jewel, beautifully carved room by beautifully carved room, carefully chalking arrows as they went to be sure they could find their way back, since every doorway in every room seemed to lead to *more* beautifully carved rooms. The Moraclada had had a house at Cleth for at least a millennium and all the time and money they needed to make the caves beneath their house (as it grew from a house to a mansion to a palace) into an elaborate, perfectly polished maze. Their artisans had not reached *all* of the cave system in the hills around Cleth, but the Below-palace was much much larger than the structure Prince Rinava had burned down.

Hence the need for the Orish Veltavan.

The farther they went, the more Ulcetha began, cautiously at first and then with increasing conviction, to believe that Trenevar (and Osmer Aidrina) was correct, and the jewels were the map through the Below-palace.

In the room that corresponded to a jade chip, Trenevar, in the lead, came to a halt so suddenly that Ulcetha crashed into him, nearly sending them both sprawling.

"What…" said Ulcetha, grabbing to make sure his glasses stayed on his face.

"*That,*" said Trenevar, pointing with an unsteady hand.

That, when Ulcetha looked, was unmistakably a dead body. Equally unmistakably, it had been here for a long time—though not long enough to be, for instance, the last prince of Cairado.

"Is that—"

"Aidrina!" said Trenevar, in what was nearly a shriek.

"Other people have gotten lost in the caves," Ulcetha said, even though he was sure Trenevar was right.

"No, look at the hair," Trenevar said, in a slightly calmer voice. "Nobody else wore first-class ribbons so old they'd faded to pink. It has to be Aidrina."

Ulcetha looked—and then looked again, his stomach contracting into a hard knot. "Is that… is that a *knife?*"

"A *knife?*" Trenevar said, his voice rising toward a shriek again.

"Someone murdered Osmer Aidrina," Ulcetha said blankly. The idea made no sense; Osmer Aidrina had been the most harmless of people—even his workmen liked him.

Trenevar swallowed hard and said, "He certainly didn't stick that knife in his own back."

"But *why?*"

"I don't know," Trenevar said.

They stared at the body silently for some time.

"What do we do?" Ulcetha asked finally. "I mean, we can't leave him here."

"Are you suggesting we turn back *now?*"

"No," Ulcetha said, although he thought maybe he should have been. "I meant on the way back. But I don't see how we can get him up the rope without him… falling apart."

"Let's save that problem for later," said Trenevar. "Aidrina won't mind waiting a little longer, and we're nearly to the end."

"Yes," Ulcetha said and looked at the Orish Veltavan, although he almost didn't need to, he'd looked at it so often in the past four hours. "Go north."

They had to step over Osmer Aidrina, and Ulcetha muttered, "Sorry," as he did so. It was a closer view than he'd wanted of the knife hilt jutting up from the middle of Osmer Aidrina's back.

"It shows that we're on the right track," Trenevar said. "Aidrina was pretty sure he knew the path, that last time."

"It would be a ghastly coincidence," Ulcetha agreed, "if Osmer Aidrina just *happened* to die in a room that was also part of the solution to the maze."

And then they came to the wall.

Trenevar had been leading quite confidently—he, after all, had been down in the Below-palace before, searching with Aidrina for the Moraclada treasure and the Orb of Cairado—and at first he said, "You must be wrong."

"I'm not wrong," Ulcetha said, handing him the Orish Veltavan. "The wire goes *that* way," and he jerked his thumb at the wall, which was carved in the honeycomb pattern the Moraclada seemed to have liked best.

Trenevar looked at the Orish Veltavan, looked at the pearl that marked their current location, and looked at the wall. "Could we have made a wrong turn earlier?"

"We've been very careful," Ulcetha said. "I mean, yes, we *could* have, but I really don't think we did."

"Could the Orish Veltavan have gotten twisted somehow?"

Ulcetha considered that. "I suppose it's *possible,* but it's pretty stiff wire, and I can't imagine anyone not being careful with it."

"Your imagination may not be good enough," Trenevar said dryly.

"Still," said Ulcetha. "Don't you think we'd be able to tell?"

"I suppose," said Trenevar. "What if we tried the rooms to either side?"

"There's been nothing in *any* of the rooms to show they matched up with the Orish Veltavan," Ulcetha said. "It seems unlikely they'd change that pattern now."

They both stood silently for some time, looking at the wall.

"Could it be a terrible joke?" Ulcetha said. "Could Prince Rinava have meant it for Edrevenivar?"

"Meaning that it's *supposed* to lead here?" Trenevar thought that over. "But then why are there jewels after the pearl? Why not just lead us to the wall and dump us?"

"Could it be…" Ulcetha could feel his face heat. "Could there be a secret door?"

"A secret door?"

"I know it's stupid," Ulcetha said hastily. "I read too many adventure novels."

"It's not stupid," Trenevar said. "It's just the sort of thing the Moraclada would do. And it makes more sense than the idea that Prince Rinava went to such extraordinary lengths for… for *nothing*. He meant the Orish Veltavan to go to his son, not to Edrevenivar."

"Why did he not destroy the Orish Veltavan, then, when his son died?"

"I imagine he was too busy burning the Summer Palace down."

"Why wasn't it destroyed in the fire? Did Osmer Aidrina ever say where he found it?"

"It had been hidden beneath a flagstone. Aidrina knew of the hiding place because I found a mention of it in Rinava's oldest daughter's diary. So it was absolutely, perfectly safe for five hundred years, until Aidrina finally moved enough rubble to uncover the correct flagstone. But all the Moraclada loved hiding places and secret passages, so a secret door is just the sort of thing they would do."

Like Mara, Ulcetha thought and shivered. "Just a second," he said. He quickly checked the room to the north and the room to the south. "Both of those rooms have blank east walls, too. So there's room."

"The question then becomes: how do we open it?"

"There must be a catch somewhere," Ulcetha said. "Maybe one of the honeycombs?"

"Maybe," Trenevar said. His ears looked daunted, but he gamely started pushing hexagons, none of which budged. Ulcetha looked at the wall, looked at the other walls, looked thoughtfully at the floor. Most of the floors in the Below-palace were simple stone, smoothed and dressed, but not elaborated on. This floor, though, had been tiled with more hexagons, *and why tile,* Ulcetha thought, *when you could simply have carved?*

He crouched down and prodded at the tiles thoughtfully.

"Do you think..." Trenevar said.

"Maybe. I mean, it *could* be." He stood up, thought for a moment, and then estimated where the middle of the floor was. That tile, when he prodded it, moved. He was able to lift it, like the lid of a box. Beneath it was a wire bent into a hook. That seemed self-evident; Ulcetha pulled it.

It took some force, but he finally heard a click, and the room's blank wall rotated outward maybe half an inch.

Trenevar was quick to pull it further out. Behind it, they found an arched doorway, identical to the doorways in the other three walls, and they stepped through into the next room, which was a chip of lapis lazuli. Its walls were garlanded with high-relief roses.

"Which way?" said Trenevar.

"Straight ahead," said Ulcetha. "East."

Between the rose quartz chip and the tourmaline chip, they had to crawl through a passage so low they could not even stay up on their hands and knees. Ulcetha was simultaneously glad he'd worn his oldest coat and terrified that the rock above them would shift and squash them into paté.

The tourmaline chip room was lavish with gilt and tourmalines, the fanciest room by far that they had found. "We must be close," said Trenevar. "Which way?"

"South," said Ulcetha. The path to the south curled back around the tourmaline room, and then curled even more tightly to the north until the path of jewels ended in a sapphire. In the cave, the path ended in a door.

It was a door that had been crafted with considerable care, just as the cave opening had been crafted with considerable care to take a door. The two fit together smoothly, without hinges on this side, a heavy wooden door (and how had they even gotten it down here?) and a smooth stone wall.

Trenevar tried the door, because someone had to, and it was locked.

"Now what?" said Ulcetha.

"Now?" said Trenevar. "Have some jerky and let's think about it."

"It's a locked door," Ulcetha said, accepting the strip of jerky Trenevar held out to him. "There isn't much to think about."

"Don't be defeatist, Zhorvena," said Trenevar.

Ulcetha bit down on the jerky instead of saying he wasn't being defeatist, and they were both silent for a while.

Finally, Trenevar, who had been examining the door, said, "This is a very peculiar looking keyhole."

Ulcetha joined him and had to agree. "It looks like it would fit the Orish Veltavan," he said, "but you couldn't turn it. The metal wouldn't hold up."

"Maybe you don't turn it," Trenevar said. "Here, let's try."

Ulcetha lined up the Orish Veltavan with the keyhole. He had to try three times before he got the right orientation, but then it slid in perfectly. He felt the tiny *chunk* as the gem chips each hit something in the lock. "Now what? I'm not going to try turning it."

"No, don't," said Trenevar. "Push. Gently."

Ulcetha pushed, very gently; there was a heavy click somewhere deep in the lock, and the door began to swing open.

"Yes!" Trenevar started forward.

"Wait!" Ulcetha yanked him back, so hard that he threw them both off balance and they ended in an untidy and painful heap on the floor.

"Wha—" Trenevar started, but they both heard the unmistakable noise of a reveth-atha (*shinnnnng-thunk!*), and looking up, saw that the door had been carefully crafted in more ways than one.

"Thank you," Trevenar said shakily after a long moment as Ulcetha tried and failed not to wonder how far through Trevenar's body the blade would have gone starting from the top of the skull. "What made you…"

"Low tastes in literature," said Ulcetha. "In adventure novels, doors to ancient treasures are always death-trapped."

"I will remember not to sneer at adventure novels," Trenevar said. "Do you think there are other traps?"

"I have no idea. Which I suppose means we had better be careful."

"Yes," Trenevar said, eyeing the reveth-atha in the doorway. "Yes, we had."

THE REVETH-ATHA MIGHT not have been the only trap in the treasury of the princes of Cairado, but it was the only one that still worked. Of course, the treasury was only one room, and not a large one—here Ulcetha's reading was at fault—containing six heavy wooden chests. They opened them one at a time, finding ingots of gold, pieces of the prince's regalia, and finally, in the fourth chest, among a careless heap of rings and necklaces, a tarnished silver scepter crowned by a spherical star sapphire as big as an egg.

"The Orb of Cairado," said Trenevar with immense, reverent satisfaction, and Ulcetha thought, *I never have to see Salathgarad again.*

WITH THE REVETH-ATHA blade in the way, the door to the treasury could no longer be closed, and there was no method that either Ulcetha or Trenevar could find of hoisting the blade back up.

"Not that one *would,*" said Trenevar, although he said it uneasily. Their return to Cairado with the Orb would be the signal for every treasure-hunter in the city to swarm Cleth, and although they could close the secret door, which would provide some protection, Ulcetha was afraid that eventually the treasure-hunters would make it to the treasure.

Trenevar was clearly thinking the same thing. He said, "We'll have to get the Department to send someone out here right away."

"Doesn't the treasure properly belong to the city?" said Ulcetha.

"It properly belongs to the descendants of the princes of Cairado," said Trenevar, "and we'd need a genealogist to tell us who those descendants *actually* are, as opposed to those who claim to be. But Osmer Harcenar has as likely a claim as anyone, if it comes to that. And you could further make the argument that, since the Department will put everything in the Museum of Cairado, it *is* going to the city. Anyone in Cairado will be able to come and look at it, and that's better than having it hidden away in a vault in the Cairad'theileian."

"You have given the matter a great deal of thought," said Ulcetha.

Trenevar shrugged. "I have been looking for the Orb of Cairado for a very long time."

"What would you do if there *was* still a prince of Cairado?"

"Well, then, it would belong to him, and trying to say otherwise would get me thrown in the Goremet," said Trenevar. "You're making this difficult, Zhorvena, and it really isn't. Not like the Barizheise Room in the Museum, where every year they get a petition from the Barizheise Museum of Culture asking for their artifacts back, and every year they send a petition to the Barizheise Museum of Culture, asking for *our* artifacts back, and nobody budges."

Ulcetha winced a little and wondered if he'd flinch at the word "artifact" for the rest of his life. "All right. But there's still the problem of Osmer Aidrina."

"Yes," said Trenevar, and some of the manic energy seemed to drain out of him. "The problem of Aidrina. We need, and I hate to say this, something to put him in. And we don't have anything."

"We can't just leave him there."

"Is that more disrespectful than picking him up and having him fall apart? Look, nothing's going to happen to him in the time it will take us to go back to Cairado and send someone out here with a basket or something."

"A *basket?*" Ulcetha protested. "Shouldn't he have a coffin?"

"A coffin will be no easier to get back to the surface. Harder, actually. And maybe I'm using the wrong word, but the Csaiveisei and the Uliseisei do have… well, baskets for transporting bodies in, bodies that are like Aidrina's and have been discovered long after death. The Ulisothala will know."

Ulcetha was not himself looking forward to touching Osmer Aidrina's body, and he suspected that was making him a coward. He said, "Are you sure—"

"Zhorvena. Aidrina was as pragmatic a person as you could hope to find. He won't visit your dreams for letting someone who knows what they're doing handle the body."

"All right, all right!" Ulcetha said, giving in. "But if he *does* visit my dreams, I'm telling him it was your idea."

"Yes," Trenevar said, and his voice caught a little. "Entirely my idea."

5

UPON LEARNING THAT both the Orish Veltavan and the Orb of Cairado had been found, the Department of History lost its collective mind. Students and scholars went racing back to the Cleth Valley with mules and baskets and miles of rope to systematically remove the treasure from the treasury (and Osmer Aidrina, finally, from the Jade Room); two scholars second-class nearly came to blows over who was going to study the regalia of the prince of Cairado first; Osmer Harcenar and Osmer Ledmenar so far forgot themselves as to gloat in public; and, possibly of interest to no one but himself, Ulcetha Zhorvena was reinstated as a scholar second-class.

There was no ceremony about it. Trenevar went with him to Osmer Harcenar's workroom, which was large and chilly and very tidy, where Osmer Harcenar looked up from the book he was reading and said, "*Really*, Trenevar?"

Ulcetha felt small and cold.

But Trenevar was undaunted. "Mer Zhorvena was of great assistance to me in finding the Orb. And I believe him when he says he did not steal the Orish Veltavan."

Osmer Harcenar raised his eyebrows. "What wonder-tale did he tell you? That he found it on the street?"

"Mer Zhorvena?"

This was the part Ulcetha had been dreading the most: having to tell the story to Osmer Harcenar. But there was no way around it; Osmer Harcenar might or might not believe him, but he certainly would not believe there was *any* innocent explanation if Ulcetha refused to talk. So he explained again, trying to tell the story coherently and not leave anything out. He was fairly sure he didn't succeed.

Osmer Harcenar stared at him thoughtfully, saying nothing. Ulcetha looked away, ears twitching wildly. He had never been able to meet Osmer Harcenar's stare. Five years of writing fake provenances had done nothing to help with that.

Trenevar said again, "He has been of great assistance to me."

Osmer Harcenar stared at him; Trenevar met his stare steadily. It was Osmer Harcenar who looked away first. "What is it you want, Trenevar?"

Trenevar said, "I agreed that if Mer Zhorvena helped me find the Orb, I would help him get reinstated. I don't think it's too much to ask."

Osmer Harcenar made a noise that might have been a laugh. "You have brought great acclaim to the Department, Trenevar, but that does not mean you own it."

"Without Mer Zhorvena's help, I would not have found the Orb."

"Of course not. He had the Orish Veltavan."

"I believe that he did not. If he'd stolen it, I don't believe he would have waited five years to pretend to find it. Five years is a long time, Harcenar."

"Are you suggesting he's done his penance?" Osmer Harcenar asked dryly.

"No, because I don't believe he's done anything wrong. And I think he's earned reinstatement, no matter what you think he did. I *also* think you owe me a favor. I could have gone straight to the museum."

The rivalry between the Department of History and the Museum of Cairado was long-standing, bitter, and (Ulcetha thought) deeply pointless. But Osmer Harcenar's loathing of Osmer Ensivar, the director of the museum, was quite real. He said, "Oh all right, Trenevar, if it will make you happy." Which was hardly an enthusiastic welcome back, but Ulcetha would take it.

A week later, dressed in his absolute best clothes and with his hair pulled sternly back, Ulcetha went with Trenevar and Osmer Harcenar to the University Senate. His heart was pounding so hard he could barely think, and the Senate chamber, with its steeply-pitched rows of desks, did not make things any better. It was like being at the bottom of a well, if a well could look at you.

He came prepared to tell his dreadful story again, but in the event it was not necessary. When their turn came in the Senate agenda, Osmer Harcenar stood up and said, "Mer Zhorvena petitions for reinstatement as a scholar second-class of the Department of History. Osmer Trenevar and I vouch for him."

The Senate President asked for discussion.

Someone near the top of the well said, "Isn't Mer Zhorvena the one who was thrown out for stealing artifacts?"

"Yes," said Osmer Harcenar, "but we are satisfied that he was falsely accused."

"After all this time?" said someone else. "It's been years."

"New evidence came to light," Osmer Harcenar said, utterly unruffled.

Ulcetha expected them to demand details, but the Senate agenda was long, and the President's patience short. He said, "Further questions?" and barely waited a beat before continuing, "Vote, please. Do we accept the reinstatement of Mer Ulcetha Zhorvena?"

The Senate voted by means of a square plaque at each desk with one face painted green and one face painted red. Turning the green face toward the President meant yes; the red face meant no. The Senate secretary (who was a staff member rather than himself a scholar) would count the reds against the greens and announce the result. It was cumbersome but meant that no senator could know how the other senators voted, which, at least in theory, kept anyone from voting simply to be with the majority.

Harcenar climbed the stairs to his own desk; Ulcetha carefully did not look to see how he voted.

The secretary seemed to take forever to count the vote, but that was partly the way Ulcetha's heart was pounding so hard he thought he might be sick. The University was all he had ever wanted, from the time he was old enough to want anything, and being without it had been like slowly starving to death while everyone around him feasted.

Finally, *finally,* the secretary said, "Yes, 23, No, 19. Yes has it."

He had no one to celebrate with—he had friends who would welcome him back, but they were also friends who had been happy to scapegoat him when the Orish Veltavan disappeared, and he discovered that he did not want to share this with Adrivar or Tesena. He certainly had no desire ever to speak to Osmer Bevanar again. He went alone to the Cat and Carpenter, where he discovered that he did not actually want to get drunk. He'd done that often enough trying to escape the shame and anger and grief?—yes, grief—of being thrown out of the Department, and it had never helped, merely leaving him with spectacular hangovers to take to Salathgarad's office in the morning.

He did celebrate enough to buy a glass of Crivoli wine instead of the house Romaki he usually contented himself with, and its sharp sweetness tasted most definitely like success.

HE HAD NOT lost the knack of braiding the blue ribbons into his hair, nor had he forgotten his ambition of trading them for the red ribbons of a scholar first-class. That meant returning to the Department, with all that *that* entailed. Everyone welcomed him back. No one apologized for throwing him out (except the elderly Osmer Sazamar, whom he had never known well). By dint of showing up in Osmer Harcenar's workroom daily, Ulcetha extracted from him a letter directing the Library Harcenada to restore his reading privileges. Likewise a letter to the University Treasurer about his stipend. With those two things restored, Ulcetha almost felt like a real scholar of the University again. But he found he was more interested in the question of who had murdered Osmer Bruna Aidrina than he was in the question of whether the prince of Cairado had held his scepter in his left hand or his right.

He was also interested in the question of who had stolen the Orish Veltavan to begin with—a question no one else was asking, since they all believed it had been him. It was *possible* that someone not in the Department had murdered Osmer

Aidrina, although he thought it very unlikely, but only a member of the Department could have stolen the Orish Veltavan, and the more he thought about it, the more he suspected that those two people—the murderer and the thief—had been the same person.

But he could not figure out why anyone would murder Osmer Aidrina, nor why anyone would steal the Orish Veltavan only to *hide* it. It almost seemed like someone wanted to keep people out of the Below-palace, but why anyone would want that—except maybe the revenant of the last prince of Cairado, and it couldn't be that, since he had burned to ashes five hundred years ago—he found himself unable to imagine.

But knowing that the murderer/thief was a member of the Department made him wary of the people who welcomed him back.

THE MEMBERS OF Dach'osmin Bruncavin's salon were delighted for him, even more delighted when he said he did not want to give the salon up, although he had to promise them he would not try to publish anything based on the research he had done in their family archives—there would be no way to hide the fact that he had had access to archives that, so far as the heads of households knew, he did not have permission to see, and that would lead to a variety of disasters. Ulcetha imagined the conversations he would end up having with Osmer Narlezar, Osmer Garmozhar, and Osmer Delbrathar, and was all too happy to comply.

HE PULLED OUT the box where, resisting the urge to just burn them, he had carefully stored all his research materials and brought them back. His carrel in the Department's main building (a sprawling collection of extensions and annexes surrounding what had once been a Thorobada mansion) had been reassigned, of course, but—mercifully—Osmer Harcenar had nothing to do with carrel assignment, and Ulcetha had been a member of the Department long enough to know that while it was officially Osmer Elivera's job, the person who really *did* assign carrels was Osmer Elivera's secretary, a University staff member named Vada Perina.

Mer Perina's desk—for he did not have as much as an office to call his own—was in the University's administration building, which had long ago been part of the same Thorobada compound as the Department. He looked up at Ulcetha's approach, a tall, habitually sad-faced man with pale gray skin and goblin orange eyes. "Mer Zhorvena!" he said. "I have been hearing a great deal about you."

"I hope none of it is too dreadful," Ulcetha said, not joking.

"Enh," said Mer Perina. "Many people do not believe that your finding of the Orish Veltavan was entirely innocent, but they are too happy about the Orb of Cairado to mind much."

"Could be worse," Ulcetha said with a sigh.

"For what it is worth, I never thought you were a thief. And since it is official that you are reinstated, people will stop talking before long."

"As long as something else comes along,"

"Something else always does," said Mer Perina. "But you must be here about your carrel."

"I am hoping there is one empty, yes."

"Oh yes," said Mer Perina. "Your Department always has more carrels than scholars, which says more about the number of carrels that have been wedged into that building than it does about history scholars. Do you want one with a piece of window or one without?"

"With," said Ulcetha, and that simply, it was done, and he was able to set himself up in an academic's fortress of library books and quires of notes. His piece of window looked out into the branches of a colmerlon tree, which was excellent for staring at when thinking of the next word, and Ulcetha thought that if he ever *did* get first-class honors and have students to teach, the first thing he would tell them was not to alienate University staff.

His first Departmental meeting back was horrid—they spent a very long time debating the question of Ulcetha's seniority: did he go back in the rankings where he had been when he was thrown out? Did the five years away count for or against him? Had he lost seniority entirely, putting him down at the bottom of the third-class scholars' tier? Trenevar spoke up for him—which Ulcetha had not been expecting, that not being part of their deal—and he ended up only at the bottom of the second-class scholars' tier, which was really the best he could hope for with Osmer Harcenar presiding. He was not nearly as exercised about seniority as he had been five years ago, since the only thing it really determined was where one got to sit at the Departmental table in the University's vast dining hall. Well, and workroom space and teaching opportunities when one became a first-class scholar, but he would worry about that when he got there.

He had been afraid that his research notes would be foreign and unknowable, and at first they were.

Then—worse—they were boring.

The policies of Edrevenivar's regents in the southern cities were all very well as a research topic, and there was certainly some value in comparing the regency of Olverhar in Cairado with Rasponar in Choharo, but the Ulcetha of five years ago had only been interested in how the regents' decisions affected the municipal governments. Ulcetha now thought that horribly dry and horribly limited, when there were much more interesting questions begging to be asked. He'd dealt with the great riots in Cairado purely in terms of how Olverhar had responded to them, but now he was much more interested in what had caused them. What had driven the citizens of Cairado to the streets and why had the citizens of Choharo not joined them? Olverhar's policies had really not differed so greatly from Rasponar's, so what had happened in Cairado that did not happen in Choharo? Or, conversely, what had happened in Choharo that failed to happen in Cairado? And what did it look like if you threw in a comparison to Nesothar's brutally repressive regime in Sevezho—so brutal that his own soldiers revolted. And they were successful where the citizens of Cairado were not. They hanged Nesothar from a renazbeth tree and put their own general, Trovimar, in his place. And Trovimar had been arguably the most successful of Edrevenivar's regents; Sevezho had become a loyal part of Edrevenivar's empire decades before either Cairado or Choharo. And that wasn't a question of municipal government at all—or, at least, he no longer thought it was. Within a week, he had scrapped a half-written draft and started all over again.

But that was all right. He would have to explain himself to the oversight committee in the fall, but by then he thought he might have enough of a draft to persuade them he was not simply failing to get any work done. And it was exciting to be doing research again, digging through the card catalogue at the Harceneise, filling out slips for books about Olverhar and Rasponar and Nesothar, wondering, though, whether the information he wanted was even in a book at all. Where did you look if you wanted to know about the motives of the sort of people historians didn't write about? He thought of one possibility and visited the archives of the Vira'theileian, the Hall of Justice, where they were very startled to be asked for the depositions from the judicial hearings into the great riots of five hundred years ago.

"But you do *have* them?" Ulcetha said.

"Certainly we have them," said the archivist, bristling. "But they are not on the shelves."

"Where are they?"

"In the storage rooms beneath the Cairad'theileian. *We* don't have room."

Ulcetha considered the size of the Vira'theileian, which covered a full city block. The archivist saw the thought on his face and said, "The last two hundred years we keep here. Everything else goes to the Cairad'theileian."

"Will they know where the depositions from the riots are?"

The archivist turned a laugh into a cough. "No, but they'll let you look for them. The municipal government values its good relationship with the University. And it's all in chronological order, so what you want should be *possible,* although it may take you some time."

"Yes, it may," Ulcetha said.

At the Cairad'theileian, they were more willing but less helpful and finally ended up simply giving him permission to go look.

The basements of the Cairad'theileian had gas lights and extremely good foundations—and since the original

Cairad'theileian had burned down during the reign of Prince Ulpava, it was *not* on the peninsula and thus not nearly as prone to flooding—and Ulcetha still had a packet of sticks of chalk in his trouser pocket from the exploration of the Below-palace. He did not hesitate to draw arrows on the floor, and soon found himself also noting dates as he tried to figure out whether the rows of shelves should be read from east to west or north to south. He also kept a close eye on his pocket-watch (redeemed from the pawn shop, and it was ridiculous how much more he felt like himself with a pocket-watch again), since there were no windows and he knew his own propensity to lose track of time when pursuing an interesting question. At six o'clock, even though he had not found the records he wanted, he made himself follow his arrows back to the stairs.

"Did you have any luck?" said the archivist as he came out.

"I'll come back," said Ulcetha.

A WEEK AFTER Osmer Aidrina's body was brought up out of the Below-palace, Osmer Sazamar, who was venerable enough not to care what Osmer Harcenar thought, petitioned a Witness for the Dead.

Her name was Steliän Mirineth; she was middle-aged, round-faced, utterly harmless-looking. She came to the Department and asked questions in a soft, nonjudgmental voice, and Ulcetha could not tell what she was thinking.

He had to tell her about finding the body, which led, of course, to the question about what he and Trenevar were doing in the Below-palace—and he had to describe the Below-palace so that she would understand why calling it merely "caves" was wrong—which led to what seemed to be a genuinely baffled question about the Orish Veltavan. So Ulcetha explained about Prince Rinava.

"I don't understand," said Min Mirineth. "If he wanted the treasure hidden, why did he make a map?"

"He wanted the treasure hidden *from Edrevenivar,*" Ulcetha said. "He most likely expected that in a decade or two, his son would be able to retrieve the Orish Veltavan and find the treasure. I don't know what he thought would happen then. But his son died fighting Edrevenivar in Vasthorno, and Prince Rinava committed suicide and brought the Summer Palace down. So the Orish Veltavan stayed lost until Osmer Aidrina found it."

"And then it was lost again."

"I didn't steal it."

"I didn't say you did. Do you have any idea who the real thief was?"

"I wish I did," Ulcetha said. "But all I've ever been able to figure out was that it had to be someone *in* the Department. And someone who for some reason doesn't want the Orb of Cairado to be found."

"But you don't know why."

"Not a clue," said Ulcetha.

6

WHEN ULCETHA GOT home, Salathgarad was on his doorstep.

"No," Ulcetha said, digging in his pocket for his key. "Whatever it is, no."

"Now, Ulcetha," said Salathgarad. "Is that any way to speak to your former employer?"

"The crucial word in that sentence is 'former.' I quit. You must have realized."

"Now, Ulcetha," Salathgarad said again. "You needn't think I hold a grudge about your quitting without notice, because I don't."

That was a lie. Salathgarad held grudges about everything.

"I don't care whether you hold a grudge or not," Ulcetha said. That was also a lie. Salathgarad could do a lot of damage if he wanted to. Salathgarad could probably get him kicked out of the University again, this time for good. But Salathgarad was a bully. If you knuckled under right away, he only browbeat you more. Ulcetha had watched him do it to a series of Barizheise clerks, none of whom lasted more than ten months. Ulcetha, however, had taken several classes with Osmer Chenovar, who was the same way, and he had stood up for himself from the first, with the result that Salathgarad merely yelled at him.

On the other hand, no one ever won a fight with Salathgarad, and Ulcetha did not delude himself that he was going to win this one. Salathgarad had too much leverage against him and knew it. He sighed. "What do you want?"

Salathgarad's smile was full of teeth. "I need you to write a provenance."

ULCETHA HAD NOT started out writing provenances for Salathgarad's fake artifact smuggling business. But Salathgarad had promised to pay him a bonus for every provenance, and a percentage of the profits for every artifact with one of his provenances that sold, and he was desperately in need of the money. Ethics and pride alike took a hard fall.

It was a simple enough matter. Salathgarad had a source for fake elven artifacts: incomplete earring sets, belt buckles, things that plausibly could have been handed down in a family for generations only to be sold in a desperate moment. Or coins. Coins with the heads of pre-Edrevenivar rulers were especially popular in Barizhan, and those someone might have found in a place like Cleth: abandoned palaces, ruined cities, temples to gods long-forgotten. Ulcetha had had his choice in making up stories about how the artifacts had reached Salathgarad's hands. He had, in a perverse way, come to enjoy it.

This time, the artifact—which Salathgarad insisted Ulcetha come back to the shop to look at—was a small hoard of coins, such as you might find tucked behind a loose brick, four with the head of Prince Rinava, the last prince of Cairado, and one with the head of Prince Ulriva, who had ruled fifty years earlier. Ulcetha felt that that last coin was a nice touch on the part of the fake-crafter; it gave the whole thing just that much more verisimilitude.

"Lots of things coming from Cleth these days," said Salathgarad, in what might have been a suggestion or an order; Ulcetha was never sure with Salathgarad. It was a good suggestion, too. Treasure hunters would be everywhere in the Cleth Valley, now that the historians had taken what they wanted and gone—a decision which Ulcetha passionately disagreed with but (Osmer Aidrina, who would have agreed with him, being dead) could do nothing about—and nothing was more plausible than that one of them would stumble across a little hoard like this.

It made the provenance very easy to write. *Found in the ruins of the Summer Palace at Cleth*. And then some dates for Prince Ulriva and Prince Rinava, and a little history about the burning of the Summer Palace and the arrival of Edrevenivar, before whom Cairado, taking good notice of her sister Vasthorno, had surrendered without a fight.

"You didn't need me for that," Ulcetha said. "What is it you're really after?"

"Well, since you're *here,*" Salathgarad said, suddenly looking shifty, and Ulcetha braced himself. "There's another artifact, but this one isn't a fake."

"I thought you only dealt in fakes," Ulcetha said. It was, in a weird backwards way, part of how he had squared things with his conscience: only fakes, not actual thefts.

"Mostly, yes," said Salathgarad. "But a friend of a friend had this thing fall into his hands and I've got a sure buyer."

"Where do I fit into this?"

"It still needs a provenance, even if it's the real thing," Salathgarad said. "We can't tell the *truth*."

"No, of course not," Ulcetha said. "What is this thing?"

"Here," Salathgarad said, going to his desk, which had, Ulcetha thought, more secret drawers than regular ones. Ulcetha did not see what Salathgarad did, nor which drawer slid open, but in a moment Salathgarad returned to the clerk's desk where Ulcetha was sitting and said, "Here."

Ulcetha stared. He knew what it was because he'd seen drawings of it in manuscripts from the reigns of Prince Armetha and Prince Ulpava.

"Where…" he said. "How…"

"The Star of Cstheio," Salathgarad said with considerable satisfaction.

Ulcetha took off his glasses to examine it more closely.

The Star of Cstheio was a diamond the size of Ulcetha's thumbnail, the same perfect blue as the Orb of Cairado, set in an elaborate silver ring, currently much tarnished. The Orb and the Star had always been considered linked gems in Cairado, ever since they had arrived in Princess Hathiän's dowry, and the gift of the Star of Cstheio to the Cairad'athmaza by Prince Altheva had been considered extremely symbolic, a sign that the mazei of the city would never turn against its prince. It was considered equally symbolic when the Star was lost, and several mazei had narrowly escaped angry crowds before the mayor and Valentis Athmaza (the successor to Corica Athmaza) had frantically invented a ceremony for the mazei to swear friendship to Cairado and its people.

"You're going to sell it?" Ulcetha blurted.

Salathgarad's eyebrows went up. "What else should I do with it?"

"It belongs to the Cairad'athmaz'are," Ulcetha said, knowing it was futile.

Salathgarad hooted with laughter. "You think I should give it back to the Cairad'athmaz'are? And what will I get in return? Sincere thanks? The mazei are as poor as a ragman's dog."

"It would be—" Ulcetha started, and bit his tongue on *the right thing to do*.

"No, my friend," said Salathgarad. "I am selling this to someone who can pay me what it's worth."

"You must not be planning to say it's the Star of Cstheio," Ulcetha said, slowly and unhappily. "Because that makes it priceless."

"We all *know* it's the Star of Cstheio," Salathgarad said. "There's no need to put it in writing."

"And that's what you want me for. A provenance for a silver ring with a cut blue diamond the size of my thumbnail."

"Exactly!"

Ulcetha considered saying, *I won't do it*. He considered saying, *I* can't *do it*. But either way, the next step—the thing they both knew and so there was no need to say—would be Salathgarad threatening to go to Osmer Harcenar and tell him exactly what Ulcetha had been doing for the past five years. He could imagine the air of injured innocence with which Salathgarad would explain that he had discovered Ulcetha was using his, Salathgarad's, perfectly upright and legal business as a blind for his, Ulcetha's, smuggling operation, and he could also imagine the satisfaction with which Osmer Harcenar would accept that story.

Once a thief, always a thief.

"All right," he said. "But I can't do it *now*. I need time to think."

"How much time?"

"A day or two," Ulcetha said. "If it's going to be plausible, there are books I need to consult."

Salathgarad gave him a long, suspicious look, but said, "All right. But not *more* than a day or two. My buyer is eager."

"Of course," Ulcetha said. "Who wouldn't be?"

7

WHAT, ULCETHA ASKED himself, a little wildly, was he going to do?

He wanted to go to Mara and talk the whole thing out. Mara might not know what to do, but he would listen without judging and without making assumptions about Ulcetha's motivations and morals. And it would help. It always helped. Except Mara was dead and could listen to nothing.

He went home, flopped down on his divan, and stared at the pressed tin ceiling. What could he do?

He could go to the Vigilant Brotherhood. He could tell them he knew where the Star of Cstheio was. And he could be locked up as a lunatic.

Try again. He could go to the Vigilant Brotherhood. He could tell them Salathgarad was in possession of an extremely valuable stolen ring. If he did not then go with them to Salathgarad's office, they wouldn't find the ring. Salathgarad's desk was too cunningly made; you had to see someone open one of the drawers before you understood how many of them there might be. If he *did* go with them, whether they found the ring or not, Salathgarad would know Ulcetha had betrayed him, and he did not fool himself that Salathgarad would not seek revenge. Salathgarad *would*.

All right. Who else could he go to? He could go to the Cairad'athmaza… and get locked up as a lunatic. And even if the Cairad'athmaza believed him, what could he do? The mazei had no power to arrest Salathgarad or search his business, although maybe they would be able to use some kind of magic to find the ring. Mazei could in novels.

But still. If the Star of Cstheio showed up anywhere right away, Salathgarad would know Ulcetha was involved because the coincidence would be too severe. But if the Star of Cstheio *disappeared…*

He found that he was looking at the fake volume on Neschonori culture in which the Orish Veltavan had been hidden. It still had its index number, making it still the safest hiding place in Cairado—if he was willing to break into the Harceneise again to put it back. He couldn't risk it falling open in a shelver's hands.

Why, he thought resentfully, *is this my problem?*

He knew the answer. It didn't have to be his problem at all. He could write a fake provenance, let Salathgarad go ahead with the sale, and watch the Star of Cstheio leave Cairado, probably never to be seen again. He knew from five years of clerking for Salathgarad that there were any number of people, elves and goblins both, who hoarded valuable things just because they were valuable. Someone like that would be ecstatic to get their hands on the Star of Cstheio and wouldn't care at all that they could never show it to anyone.

And Ulcetha found, to his own deep irritation, that he found that scenario horrifying. Trenevar's argument about the Orb of Cairado had made sense; the Orb, after all, was going to stay in Cairado, in the Museum where it could be seen and studied and remain part of Cairado's culture. But this was different. The Star wouldn't even go to a museum, and it certainly wouldn't be where the people of Cairado could see it. And besides, the Star belonged to the Cairad'mazan'theileian, and nothing he said to himself could shake the belief that, even if he couldn't give it back right away, he had to keep it *possible* for the mazan'theileian to have it again.

He wished Mara was alive to talk him out of it.

THERE WAS NO point in waiting. Just after midnight, he put his black and plum scarf over his head, took his adjustable lantern, and set out, not happily, for Salathgarad's shop.

The front door was locked, but the back door had a fatal flaw Salathgarad did not know about and none of his clerks had ever told him. If you hit the door just right, it juddered the latch free of the jamb. No need to use a key at all. And from so many clerks doing that so many times, as a piece of petty spite that Salathgarad would never know about and thus never retaliate for, there was a quite noticeable dent just where you needed to hit. He let himself in, adjusted the lantern, and approached Salathgarad's massive desk.

He knew it was full of secret drawers. He knew how one or two of them worked, but he suspected he would not find the Star of Cstheio in either of them and he was correct. Grimly he began taking drawers out, feeling behind each of them for catches or buttons. He found a number of places Salathgarad had hidden things—including some pornographic photographs that made him blush to the roots of his hair—but did not find the Star. And really, he thought, sitting on the floor amid all the desk drawers, he was going at this the wrong way. Salathgarad hadn't taken a drawer out to get at the Star of Cstheio. It had to be…

Ulcetha crawled under the desk, feeling at the sides and across the top, searching for something to push or pull. He found a tiny trap door in the top of the desk, opened it with some careful prodding, and was just in time to catch the Star of Cstheio before it hit the floor.

On his way out, leaving drawers everywhere so it would be obvious the person who found the Star had not known where to search (which was even true), and taking the valuable things he had found so it would not be quite so obvious that he had known the Star was there, he carefully shut the back door again. The latch squeaked against the doorframe, but Ulcetha had done this before and knew to give it a good hard jerk, and sure enough it came back into place.

And at that moment, a voice said from the street, "Is someone there?"

This was not a residential neighborhood, but there were night watchmen in several of the warehouses on Prince Altheva Street, and blessed goddesses, one of them must have heard something. Ulcetha, the Star of Cstheio suddenly burning against his thigh, did not wait to find out if the man would go away, or if he could talk his way out of trouble. He turned in the other direction and bolted like a rabbit.

LIKE A RABBIT, Ulcetha knew the tunnels of his warren—the warren in this case being the streets between Salathgarad's shop and his own apartment. He stuck to the alleyways until he reached Hazenthar Avenue, but there were enough people around—delivery men and prostitutes and opera-goers—that he was able, whisking the plum and black scarf off his head, to step out among them and look like nothing more than a clerk who'd been out too late drinking at the Koi Pond or the Green Dish or one of the other fancy bars along Hazenthar Avenue.

If anyone had been chasing him, which as far as he could tell they had not. And when he thought about it, a night watchman who left his post to chase a possible thief might very well be fired, whether he caught the thief or not, and a man would have to be a fool to risk a good job for a noise that only *might* be a thief.

A fool or a lot fonder of Salathgarad than anyone on Prince Altheva Street had any reason to be.

HE HAD TO go back to his apartment and get the book-box, which was not of a convenient size to lug all over the city, and this gave him an opportunity which he thought even Osmer

Aidrina would have been hard-pressed to pass up: he tried on the ring.

It did not fit him—the last Cairad'athmaza to wear it must have had big hands—but, even tarnished, it was a beautiful ring, and just for a second he let himself admire it on his hand. Then he took it off, wrapped it in the black and plum scarf, and put it in the book ostensibly on the Neschonori. And then he set out for the Harceneise.

IT WAS EASIER the second time.

HE WAS PUTTING the book back on the shelf when the flaw in his plan occurred to him. There *was*, in fact, someone else in the city who knew the secret of the book. They must know by now—unless they were dead—that the Orish Veltavan had been found. It seemed unlikely that they would check back, but they *could*. And depending on the circles they moved in, they might hear that the Star of Cstheio was missing, since he doubted Salathgarad's ability to keep his mouth shut about it. Was it probable that they would put two and two together and get four? He found that he had no idea. He had no idea how this person's mind worked. Why steal the Orish Veltavan and then just hide it? Why not sell it through someone like Salathgarad? Why not use it to find the Orb of Cairado? What good did hiding it do you?

He was hiding the Star of Cstheio, because he did not dare let Salathgarad know he was the thief. He considered that on his way back down through the Harceneise. Was the thief someone who couldn't afford to be known as the thief? Well, that would be true of anyone in the Department, and it was still true that *only* someone in the Department could have stolen the Orish Veltavan.

So this was someone who didn't *want* to sell the Orish Veltavan, because you could do that anonymously—or anonymously enough. But if they didn't want to sell it, why steal it? Anyone in the Department could have come and spent as much time with the Orish Veltavan as they wanted. Announce it was your research specialty, and no one would look at you twice. So it wasn't *just* the Orish Veltavan. It was someone, as he had thought when deciding that this person had also murdered Osmer Aidrina, who did not want the Orb of Cairado found. But, no, that was nonsense, too. If that was what you wanted, why not *destroy* the Orish Veltavan? Or bend it. Twist it. Make it useless. It would have been terrifyingly easy for this person to have done that.

So it wasn't that they didn't want it found at all. And then he felt like his mind turned a corner to find the truth waiting for him: the thief-murderer was someone who wanted to be the one to find the Orb of Cairado. Steal the Orish Veltavan so no one else can make progress. Murder Osmer Aidrina when it looked like he was getting too close. But then, he turned another corner, you'd hamstrung yourself. Because how could you find the Orb of Cairado without admitting that you were the one who had the Orish Veltavan?

He barely noticed walking home as he tried to get this new idea to settle with the rest of what he knew. It made sense. It made far more sense than someone not wanting the Orb found at all. *And* it suggested a person, although he tried hard not to make that connection final, because everybody knew who the person in the Department who most wanted to find the Orb was. Osmer Vora Trenevar.

Had he really taken the Orish Veltavan straight to the person who had stolen it? The thought made him writhe. And then made him shudder at how lucky he was Trenevar hadn't decided to murder *him*. But he saw after a second that the two cases were not the same. Osmer Aidrina, if he had succeeded, would have had sole credit for finding the Orb of Cairado. Ulcetha, disgraced and desperate, had been perfectly happy to let Trenevar take the credit for the find, although someone else might have insisted on sharing fifty-fifty. Ulcetha did not even *want* credit, except insofar as it persuaded Osmer Harcenar to clear him to the University Senate. He could not have been a more perfect chicken for Trenevar's plucking.

Be grateful, he thought. *It is why thou art still alive.* Osmer Aidrina must have been, in Trenevar's estimation, getting too close. *But they were friends!* a part of him protested, the part that wanted to believe the best of everybody.

Yes, said a more cynical part. *Osmer Aidrina told Trenevar everything.*

Everything.

8

He was woken before dawn by a ferocious pounding on his door.

Ulcetha got up, his braided hair flopping down his back, and put his glasses on. "Who is it?" he called, knowing the answer.

"Salathgarad," snarled Salathgarad through the door.

"What do you want?" Ulcetha said, trying to sound bewildered.

"My *diamond*. Let me in or I will, I swear by all the gods, kick your door down."

"Your diamond?" Ulcetha said, still (he hoped) sounding bewildered. "What are you talking about?"

"Let me *in,* Ulcetha."

Ulcetha had been weighing the advisability of opening the door. It was a bad idea, but he believed Salathgarad when he said he would kick the door down, and that was probably worse.

Ulcetha opened the door.

Salathgarad shoved in, grabbing Ulcetha by the front of his pajamas, and slammed him up against the wall. "Where is my diamond?"

Ulcetha wheezed for breath. "I don't know what you're talking about."

"Someone stole my diamond last night, and I can't help noticing that you were the last person I showed it to."

"Someone *stole* the Star of Cstheio?" Ulcetha said and managed, he thought, to sound horrified.

Salathgarad's grip tightened. "Someone who knew my desk has secret drawers in it went through them all."

"Salathgarad, *everyone* knows your desk has secret drawers in it, starting with every clerk you've ever had."

"Look," said Salathgarad, "give it back and we can pretend this never happened."

That was a lie. Ulcetha answered it with a lie of his own: "I don't have it."

Salathgarad eyed him suspiciously. "I don't," Ulcetha said. "I have no idea where it is or who took it. Except that it wasn't me."

"Then you wouldn't object to, say, my searching your apartment?"

"I would object, actually," Ulcetha said, truthful this time, but grateful he'd left the other valuables from Salathgarad's desk cached behind the Neschonori book. "But it's not like I can stop you."

"True," said Salathgarad and let him go. Ulcetha thumped back down off his tiptoes. And watched while Salathgarad searched his apartment.

He was not a barbarian about it. He did not throw things around; he did not break anything. He had clearly done this sort of thing before. He was thorough and methodical. And he did not find the Star of Cstheio.

"Well?" Ulcetha said. He knew his ears were flat, but that would read as anger.

"It's not here," Salathgarad said. He sounded baffled.

"No, because *I didn't take it*."

"But who else could it be?" Salathgarad asked, which was hardly flattering.

"You'd know better than I would," Ulcetha said.

Salathgarad scowled at him. "If I find out it *was* you…"

"It *wasn't*."

Salathgarad stood a moment longer, clearly wanting to find a way to leave without admitting defeat, then simply turned and walked out.

Ulcetha listened to him thumping down the stairs, then the bang of the front door. Only then did he let himself sit down on the divan, shuddering with reaction. Salathgarad could quite easily have chosen to beat him up, just because, and might have chosen to do worse, if he hadn't believed Ulcetha's lies.

Thou art a fool, Ulcetha said to himself and fell back to lie across the divan, staring at the ceiling and trying to figure out what he was going to do about the Star of Cstheio. Or Trenevar. Or, ideally, both.

The trouble was, he had no proof. No proof that he hadn't stolen the Orish Veltavan to begin with, no proof that Trenevar was a murderer. No proof for that matter that he hadn't stolen the Star of Cstheio because, oh, wait a minute, he *had*. That he'd stolen it from Salathgarad, who was the next best thing to a thief himself, seemed somewhat unfortunately beside the point.

He decided the best thing to do was leave the Star of Cstheio alone for a while. Salathgarad would suspect him all over again when it was returned to the Cairad'athmaz'are, but the longer there was between the theft and the restoration, the more other people it would have occurred to him to suspect. And it was quite safe where it was. Trenevar knew the Orish Veltavan wasn't there. He had no reason to go back.

Unless he stole something else and wanted to hide it.

He wouldn't, though. It was the Orb of Cairado that Trenevar was a little bit insane about, not anything else, and the Orb was safely in the Museum of Cairado where it (at least arguably) belonged.

Besides, he knew that Ulcetha had found his hiding place. He wouldn't use it again.

So the Star of Cstheio was safe, at least for the time being. The real question was what he was going to do about Trenevar.

Nothing was certainly the safest answer, and for several days, back in the basements of the Cairad'theileian, he thought he was going to be able to live with it. He found the depositions for the judicial hearings about the great riots, and he sat on the floor there in the basement and read them, taking page after page of notes, learning the answers to questions he would never even have thought to ask. And the causes of the great riots were clarified and obscured and clarified again, and Ulcetha wanted nothing more than to forget about other matters and simply pursue this five-hundred-year-old question.

But at the same time, he didn't want Trenevar to get away with theft (letting Ulcetha himself take the blame, at that) and murder. He had liked Osmer Aidrina, who never quite seemed in focus unless he was talking about the Orb of Cairado, and it was *that* he found himself thinking about at night, not his own research. Ulcetha did not delude himself that he could make any claim to be an ethical person—not after working for Salathgarad for five years—but even so. Murder was wrong, whether he had liked Osmer Aidrina or not. Whether he liked Trenevar or not. Murder was wrong, no matter what the consequences might be of finding the murderer—and consequences there would be. He didn't delude himself about that, either. He might not ruin himself academically (it would depend on how many of the scholars first-class had *also* liked Osmer Aidrina), but he would ruin himself for sure and all with Csecoro. How could anyone maintain any kind of relationship with the person who got their brother beheaded?

And he might yet be wrong. His theory made sense and fit the facts, but that didn't necessarily mean it was correct. There might be other facts he didn't know. There might be a way of looking at the facts that he hadn't seen. If he was wrong, all this agonizing was unnecessary and pointless, and he could go back to his depositions.

He didn't think he was wrong.

Finally, sleeplessly, he decided the best thing to do was go and tell the whole story to Min Mirineth. She was the Witness for Bruna Aidrina; maybe she had found something that would prove the truth of Ulcetha's theory. Or maybe she had found something that would prove Ulcetha's theory was a pile of nonsense. Either way would be better than what he had now.

Min Mirineth, being a judicial Witness for the Dead rather than a Witness *vel ama,* had an office in the Vira'theileian, which she shared with three other Witnesses. They were all there when Ulcetha knocked on the door, but Min Mirineth looked at his face and the set of his ears and said, "Mer Zhorvena, would you like privacy for this conversation?"

"Yes," said Ulcetha, and the other three Witnesses good-naturedly gathered up their things and left.

"Pray be seated," said Min Mirineth, "and tell me how I can help."

Ulcetha told her the whole story, starting with Mara and even including the Star of Cstheio, the theft of which (if it *was* theft, taking it from someone who had no right to it) was outside her remit as Witness for Bruna Aidrina. Min Mirineth listened intently, not interrupting, and when he was done made him go back over certain pieces of the story, most particularly the pieces that made him think the murderer was Trenevar.

"It's nonsense, isn't it?" Ulcetha said, almost pleading.

"No," said Min Mirineth, "it isn't nonsense. You've given a *reason* for Osmer Aidrina to be killed, which no one else I've talked to has been able to do."

"But I have no proof. It's just my story against Osmer Trenevar's story."

"Thus far, Osmer Trenevar hasn't *told* a story," Min Mirineth pointed out. "He professed himself utterly baffled by Osmer Aidrina's murder."

"What did he say about the Orish Veltavan?"

"He said that you had come to him with it—he did quite faithfully repeat the story, for his version matched what you told me, but I admit he was very noncommittal about whether he believed you or not."

"It is a lunatic's story, I know that."

"That doesn't make it untrue. Frankly, I think if you *had* stolen the Orish Veltavan, you would have come up with a better story about finding it."

"Thank you, I think," said Ulcetha, and Min Mirineth smiled at him.

"In any event," she said, "the theft of the Orish Veltavan is not in my remit, except insofar as it is linked to the murder of Bruna Aidrina. Which your theory suggests it is. I will go back to the Department of History and ask questions about the Orish Veltavan."

"They'll all tell you I stole it."

"Maybe. But that tells me only that that it is a useful belief. Not that it is true. Witnesses know better than to believe what people tell us."

"Have you talked to Osmin Trenevin?"

"Osmin Trenevin? No, I have not."

"She is very close to Osmer Trenevar. If anyone would know something… *anything*, it would be her."

"I will talk to her," said Min Mirineth, "but persuading a sister to give information that will get her brother executed is not easy."

"Maybe if I came with you?" said Ulcetha, grimly aware that he was only making things worse for himself but also aware that he was already committed to this line of action and there was no point in being half-hearted about it. "We are friends. And she believed me when I told her I had been framed for the theft of the Orish Veltavan."

Min Mirineth regarded him, ears cocked thoughtfully. "It is an unusual but not unprecedented step. Very well. We will talk to Osmin Trenevin together."

9

The Trenevada lived on the peninsula, between the Second and Third Walls. The house was not large enough to be a compound, but the grounds were extensive, as the Trenevada had lived here since before the Third Wall was built. Csecoro, who was always home, even if somewhat unattentive, to guests in the afternoons, welcomed Ulcetha and Min Mirineth with a puzzled smile. "Mer Zhorvena, how pleasant to see you! But who have you brought me?"

"Osmin Trenevin," Ulcetha said, "this is Min Mirineth, the Witness for Bruna Aidrina. She wishes to speak with you briefly."

Csecoro looked even more puzzled. "Of course. But I don't know what I can tell you. I only met Osmer Aidrina a handful of times."

"Really, there's only one question," said Min Mirineth. She produced a wrapped bundle from inside her coat and unwrapped it deftly. "Do you know this knife?"

Csecoro looked, and they all knew the moment she recognized it. One hand crept to cover her mouth. "Is that…"

"The knife used to murder Osmer Aidrina?" Min Mirineth said, not unsympathetically. "Yes, it is."

Ulcetha watched as Csecoro pulled herself up, pulled herself together, and said, "Yes. It belongs to my brother. It has been missing from his study for four years. He told me he broke it."

"Ah," said Min Mirineth. "I think that's the only question I needed to ask. Thank you, Osmin Trenevin."

Csecoro said to Ulcetha, "I will *never* forgive thee."

"I know," he said. "I'm sorry."

She stared at him for a moment as he realized just how completely that had been the wrong thing to say—*he* had been living with the necessity of betraying her for a week, but *she* had not—then slapped him hard across the face. "We think it would be better if you left now," she said coldly.

He nodded, jerked his glasses back into place, and turned to follow Min Mirineth out of the house.

MUCH TO HIS somewhat numb surprise, Min Mirineth stopped at the first tea-house they came to and said with great firmness, "I am buying you a cup of tea."

He followed her into the River-Maiden's Mirror and obediently sat at the only free table with her. He managed to say, "This is very kind, but you really don't—"

"Yes, I do, though," said Min Mirineth. "You did something very difficult and got an answer I am sure you did not want."

"No, I didn't want it to be Osmer Trenevar. I *still* don't want it to be Osmer Trenevar, but there isn't—"

The server, a part-goblin girl with a thick coronet of ink-black braids, came up and said, "Good afternoon. What is your pleasure?"

Min Mirineth said, "A two-cup pot of golden orchor, and I think a plate of kismitrai."

"Of course," said the server, and if she was surprised that it was the woman who gave the order, she did not show it.

"This is the ugliest part of my job," said Min Mirineth. "For the most part, I enjoy what I do, but it is never pleasant to show a person's family that they are a murderer."

"No."

"Min Trenevin is a brave and honest woman. And she may yet forgive you."

"How can she?" Ulcetha said bleakly. "I put her in the position of betraying her brother, and almost certainly to his death. Unless you think there's a chance of clemency?"

"It seems unlikely," Min Mirineth said. "A premeditated murder—premeditated, for why else would he have had that wicked knife with him?—and for what? What were Osmer Trenevar and Osmer Aidrina in competition *for*?"

"Ah," said Ulcetha. "It is difficult to explain, for I am not sure I understand it myself."

"Try," said Min Mirineth.

"The Orb of Cairado… if I say they were in competition for academic honor, that doesn't at all convey what was going on. They were both obsessed with the Orb—they'd both spent twenty years trying to find it, Osmer Aidrina in the ruins of the Summer Palace, Osmer Trenevar in the diaries of Prince Rinava's courtiers."

"How…?"

"He thought one of them might have written down the secret of the Moraclada treasury. Which as it turns out would have been all but impossible, but you can't know that going in. He got a number of monographs out of his research, just never the thing he sought. And Osmer Aidrina was out at Cleth, using his own money when the Department wouldn't fund him any farther, not publishing a thing and everyone in the Department making jokes about him, and *he* was the one who found the Orish Veltavan."

"It doesn't sound like Osmer Aidrina was very interested in academic honor."

The server returned with a tray holding the teapot, two cups, the tiny hourglass that showed how long the tea had to steep, and two forks with the plate of kismitrai—a Barizheise pastry, flaky and crisp and drenched in honey, and one of Ulcetha's weaknesses.

"Min Mirineth," he said, trying one more time, "this really isn't—"

"Have a kismitris," Min Mirineth suggested. "And tell me about Osmer Aidrina."

Ulcetha gave in. The kismitris tasted like afternoon sunlight. He said, "You're right. Osmer Aidrina didn't care about academic honor. He didn't care that he had the smallest workroom in the Department or that he was never asked to teach. He wanted to find the Orb, and I don't know whether it was something about the Orb itself or something else… solving the puzzle, maybe? Knowing for his own satisfaction that he was the one who found the Orb? I never really understood Osmer Aidrina. I don't think anybody did—except maybe Osmer Trenevar."

"I have been told they were friends," Min Mirineth said, although she sounded dubious. She poured the tea, which was approximately the same color as the kismitrai.

"Yes," said Ulcetha. "I mean, yes, it's true. They were very close."

"But in competition."

"I'm not sure Osmer Aidrina noticed that part. He was tremendously observant about the ruins of the Summer Palace and then about the Orish Veltavan, but not very observant about people. And Osmer Trenevar couldn't entirely hide his own obsession with the Orb of Cairado, but I think he did a good job of hiding how deep it went. And he *did* care about whether he had a good workroom and whether he was asked to teach and whether he had any power in the Department."

"And would finding the Orb of Cairado mean he got the things he wanted?"

"Oh yes," said Ulcetha, thinking of that conversation with Osmer Harcenar. He took a sip of tea—more delicate than black orchor, but still bracing—and ate another kismitris.

Min Mirineth took a kismitris for herself. "So Osmer Trenevar wanted to find the Orb of Cairado for what it would mean to his career, but Osmer Aidrina just wanted to find the Orb. Is that...?"

"Accurate," said Ulcetha. "Although I think Osmer Trenevar also wanted to find the Orb for the sake of finding the Orb. He could have gotten the academic honor he wanted in any number of ways."

"Did anyone else in the Department feel this obsession? Did you?"

"Me?"

"You found the Orish Veltavan. You found the Orb just as much as Osmer Trenevar did."

"But I didn't..." He drank more tea to stall for time. "I didn't set out to do any of that."

"Do you not want academic honor?"

The question sounded sincere, and Ulcetha couldn't help a harsh snort of laughter. "It doesn't matter whether I want it or not, I'm never going to get it. I'm just grateful the Department let me back in."

"They had no reason not to."

"You don't know Osmer Harcenar. He never liked me to begin with."

"Why not?"

Trust a Witness to ask the uncomfortable question. Ulcetha said, "I'm a shopkeeper's son. Zhorvena, not Zhorvenar. Osmer Harcenar thinks history should be written *by* the same sort of people it's written *about*." It occurred to him that he was, in his own way, proving Osmer Harcenar right—a shopkeeper's son writing about shopkeepers—and just how much Osmer Harcenar was going to hate that.

But that was most definitely a problem for another day. He said, "Osmer Harcenar likes Osmer Trenevar, though. There have started to be whispers that he might put forward Osmer Trenevar as his successor when—*if*—he finally cedes control of the Department to someone else."

"So Osmer Trenevar has been getting everything he wanted."

"Yes," Ulcetha said. "Until I ruined it."

"*You* are not the murderer," said Min Mirineth. "The responsibility for ruining Osmer Trenevar's career rests with Osmer Trenevar."

"Does telling yourself that actually work?"

"It takes practice," said Min Mirineth. "But it is the truth."

THE HEARING BEFORE the judiciar Lord Ospragar into the murder of Bruna Aidrina took place a week after Min Mirineth made her deposition. Some judiciars made their decisions based solely on written depositions; others liked to hear the Witnesses' testimony. There was great debate among judicial scholars about which method was to be preferred, but all that really mattered as far as Ulcetha was concerned was that Lord Ospragar liked to hear testimony for himself. Ulcetha was required to attend, in case there were questions about the finding of Osmer Aidrina's body, and it was as miserable a duty as attending the Department meeting where they had ceremonially demanded his keys back and thrown him out as a thief.

He got no sleep the night before.

That morning, he dressed carefully, braided the second-class ribbons into his hair carefully, tried to lose himself in petty details, but ended up watching the hands crawl on the face of his pocket watch for the torturous hours from dawn to the earliest moment he could reasonably start walking to the Vira'theileian.

He took the longest route, walked slowly, made himself stop for breakfast at the Chandler Street zhoän even though he could hardly persuade himself he was hungry. He was still painfully early, and ended up walking slow laps around the Vira'theileian until he could go in without looking like he was avid for Trenevar's ordeal, which he was not. But finally when he looked at his watch, it told him it was a quarter to nine, and he was able to climb the Vira'theileian's great marble staircase and go inside.

The Vira'theileian was one of the oldest buildings in Cairado; it had survived at least three major fires and who knew how many architectural fads. The atrium soared three stories to the roof, stained glass windows admitting both light and color, and the dome of the rotunda rose at least three more. There were stairs that would take an intrepid visitor to the top of the dome, though Ulcetha had never climbed them. And he wasn't going to do so today.

Instead, he followed the signs to the third eshen'theileian, which had a sign on the door: OSMER VORA TRENEVAR. Wishing mightily to be anywhere else—even Salathgarad's horrible shop seemed inviting by comparison—Ulcetha pushed the door open and went inside.

The eshen'theileian was a long narrow room, with rows of wooden chairs like a neighborhood opera association's makeshift theater. There was a dais at the far end of the room which had a horseshoe of tables, open end toward the audience, three chairs on each side and one chair at the back that obviously belonged to the judiciar. The amber and cranberry carpet on the floor was beginning to show wear, and Ulcetha wondered, mind gripping frantically after any topic other than the relevant one, how often it had to be replaced.

He had spared himself the indignity of being the first person there. Csecoro had arrived, with Neliän Mulabin for support, sometime while he was picking his way through the snarl of alleys behind the Vira'theileian, and was seated at the front of the room. Both women looked back at the door as Ulcetha came in and then looked pointedly away, Osmin Mulabin with a dismissive little ear flip that made his face heat. He took a seat in the back row of chairs and tried to become invisible.

The room filled slowly: clerks and Witnesses, newspapermen and the curious. A small contingent of Trenevar's students from the Department, who also made a point of ignoring Ulcetha. No one with better than third-class ribbons showed up, other than Ulcetha himself, which said something about the Department Ulcetha wasn't sure he wanted to decipher. Trenevar's colorless little wife, whose name Ulcetha could not remember, did not come with Csecoro, but with two men who so strongly resembled her they had to be her brothers—from which Ulcetha deduced that she had fled the House Trenevada and returned to her own.

At nine o'clock precisely, the door at the back of the room opened and Lord Ospragar came in, followed by two members of the Vigilant Brotherhood escorting Trenevar, followed by the Witness for Bruna Aidrina and the Witness for Vora Trenevar. The Witnesses, Min Mirineth and a tall, gaunt man in an old-fashioned wig, looked appropriately solemn. Trenevar looked like he, too, had had a sleepless night. Everyone sat down, Min Mirineth alone on the right, and Trenevar and his Witness together on the left, the Brothers standing behind them. Ulcetha saw Trenevar glance sideways at his sister, and she at once got up and came to the table where he was sitting. The Brothers exchanged a glance and decided to allow it. Csecoro leaned over the table, and she and Trenevar had a whispered conversation that looked like he was trying to persuade her to go home and she wasn't budging. She touched his hands where he had them folded on the table as if it were an embrace and returned to her seat. Osmin Mulabin put an arm around her and they leaned together.

There was no one in Cairado who would do as much for Ulcetha. He felt cold and very lonely.

"Let us begin," said Lord Ospragar, who had a high, nasal, finicky voice. "We will hear the Witness for Bruna Aidrina."

Min Mirineth rose and bowed to Lord Ospragar. She then explained Osmer Bruna Aidrina, calmly, compassionately, and as fully as anyone could who had never spoken to him. She seemed to have grasped the depth of his obsession with the Orb of Cairado, for she finished by saying, "He would *never* have stopped searching."

"And for Vora Trenevar?" said Lord Ospragar.

The other Witness rose and said, "Vora Trenevar has requested to witness for himself."

A little murmur wound through the hearing room. The newspapermen all looked suddenly twice as interested. "That is his right," Lord Ospragar said, although he sounded dubious. "Very well."

Trenevar rose. He said, "We thank you, Lord Ospragar, for granting our request." And then he began: "We were friends with Bruna Aidrina for many years. We shared an obsession, although he pursued it in the ruins of the Summer Palace and we pursued it through the records of the reign of Prince Rinava and the diaries of his courtiers. We would meet periodically and share the results of our researches, more for the comfort of talking to someone who understood than for the sake of any progress either of us was making. But we celebrated when Aidrina found the Orish Veltavan, and we listened to his theories about what it was and how to read it. But it seemed no more fruitful than our endless diaries… until he uncovered the door to the Below-palace, and suddenly he had," Trenevar made an odd, frustrated little gesture, "he had somewhere he could *apply* his theories. And we knew that what Witness Mirineth said was true. He would never stop searching. He would find the Orb of Cairado.

"We confess, Lord Judiciar, that we lost our head. All we could think about was how to sabotage Aidrina, how to make it impossible for him to find the Orb of Cairado before we did. We stole the Orish Veltavan—and although we did not intend it, we did nothing to correct the belief that it was Ulcetha Zhorvena who took it—and we hid it in the Library Harcenada. Without it, we thought that no one could find the Orb, for we had been in the Below-palace often enough to know how vast it is, and Aidrina's methodical explorations would take *years*. But we reckoned without Bruna Aidrina. He had taken notes about the Orish Veltavan, he had drawn it from a number of different angles, he had measured everything he could possibly measure. And he *recreated* it, not in wire and jewels, but in his head. He recreated it and he was following it—slowly and with many wrong turns, but he was following it, and we thought he would certainly succeed. We now think that the secret door might have baffled him into thinking his notes were wrong, but that is neither here nor there. We believed he would find it, and we could not bear it.

"So we killed him. We lied to our wife and sister about where we were going. We followed him out to Cleth, where he was happy to see us. We followed him into the Below-palace and listened as he explained the progress he was making, and when he bent over his notebook to determine where he should go next, we drew out our knife and stabbed him. He fell and we thought him dead, but we dragged him two rooms away before we climbed out of the Below-palace, and when we found him with Mer Zhorvena, he was in the room we stabbed him in. So he must have crawled back there and died trying to get one room closer to the Orb."

"But how did you then come to find the body?" said Lord Ospragar.

"Mer Zhorvena found the Orish Veltavan and brought it to us."

"How did Mer Zhorvena come to find the Orish Veltavan?" said Lord Ospragar. "Is Mer Zhorvena here?"

Reluctantly, Ulcetha stood up. "We are here."

"Come forward," said Lord Ospragar, "and explain how you found this thing that Osmer Trenevar had hidden."

Even more reluctantly, Ulcetha walked to the front of the

room and bowed to Lord Ospragar. And told his ridiculous story, wincing as Lord Ospragar's eyebrows rose higher and higher.

"Indeed," said Lord Ospragar when Ulcetha had finished. "But how did Mer Lilana come to have this index number?"

"We have no idea," said Ulcetha.

"Osmer Trenevar?"

Trenevar wrung his hands and said, "We do not know."

"Come now," said Lord Ospragar. "One of you must know." There was a long silence while he stared at Trenevar, who was visibly starting to tremble. Finally Lord Ospragar said, softly, "Did you know Mara Lilana, Osmer Trenevar?"

And Trenevar said, every bit as reluctant as Ulcetha, "We were lovers."

Osmerrem Trenevaran gasped.

"Lovers!" said Lord Ospragar. "But how did you meet?"

"At Mer Zhorvena's second-class honors ceremony," said Trenevar. "It was… it was the strangest experience of my life. As soon as I saw Mara, I had to speak to him. As soon as I spoke to him, I had to touch him. As soon as I touched him, I had to kiss him. And it was the same for him. Neither of us was strong enough to resist it, whatever it was, even though both of us were married. We were still lovers when he died on the *Wisdom of Choharo*, and we would still have been lovers if we both lived to be ninety. The attraction between us was that strong."

"But he read your diary."

"He must have," said Trenevar. "We certainly did not tell him that index number. He read our diary and gave Mer Zhorvena the index number in that very odd and roundabout way. But he said nothing to us at any time about the Orish Veltavan."

"He wouldn't," said Ulcetha.

“Mer Zhorvena?” said Lord Ospragar.

“Mer Lilana hated conflict,” Ulcetha said. “He didn’t even like bokh. It was too antagonistic. He would never either have admitted to Osmer Trenevar that he had read his diary nor have accused him of being the thief of the Orish Veltavan, even though he knew that the accusation had destroyed my career.”

“But why did he not come to you directly?” said Lord Ospragar.

“Because,” said Ulcetha, who had had time to think this through, “if he told us he knew where the Orish Veltavan was, he would either have to refuse to tell us how to find it, which we promise would have caused a horrendous row, or admit that he was Osmer Trenevar’s lover. And if he told us, he would have to tell everyone who wanted to know how we found the Orish Veltavan if we weren’t the thief in the first place. So for Mer Lilana, a paper chase that only started after he was dead would seem perfect.”

“But why did he read our diary?” The question seemed to burst out of Trenevar.

“It was a secret,” Ulcetha said, hating that his answer was not better. “Mara—Mer Lilana loved finding out secrets. We used to joke that he should have been the historian, since that’s really all the study of history is.”

“He betrayed me,” Trenevar said and put his face in his hands.

Ulcetha felt more than slightly betrayed himself. That Mara had valued his own comfort over Ulcetha’s entire life was… a little horrifying. Ulcetha supposed he should be grateful that Mara had cared enough about their friendship to leave him the clues he had. He wondered if Mara would ever have given that envelope to him *without* having died first.

“Very well,” said Lord Ospragar. “Osmer Trenevar, have you anything else to say?”

"No," Trenevar said without looking up.

"Witness Plasthovar?"

"No," said the Witness in the old-fashioned wig. "Osmer Trenevar has told the truth."

"Witness Mirineth, have you anything to add?"

"No," said Min Mirineth.

"Then our judgment is that Osmer Vora Trenevar is guilty of the murder of Osmer Bruna Aidina and shall be executed by the reveth-atha one week from today."

"Lord Ospragar!" It was Csecoro, who had shoved to her feet.

Lord Ospragar looked at her, eyebrows raised.

Undaunted, she said, "We would beg clemency for Osmer Trenevar. He is the only adult male of the House Trenevada in Cairado, and his heir is a child of three."

"That is unfortunate," said Lord Ospragar, "but it is not much to weigh in the scales against murder."

"He is a scholar first-class."

"So was his victim."

"Surely it is obvious that he will not murder again."

"Not until he finds a new obsession," said Lord Ospragar. "Can you swear that he will not?"

She tried. But her ears flattened slowly, and finally she shook her head.

"Our judgment stands," said Lord Ospragar. He stood up and walked out, the two Witnesses following him.

Csecoro dropped back into her chair and put her face in her hands, mirroring her brother.

Osmerrem Trenevaran was crying.

The Brothers stepped forward and pulled Trenevar to his feet.

Ulcetha, frankly, fled.

Over the next week, he got letter after letter from the members of Dach'osmin Bruncavin's salon. Most of them were rescinding his permission to use their family archives; Dach'osmin Bruncavin wrote that, while she honored him for making such a difficult choice, it might be better if he did not return to the salon. Only Osmin Narlezin wrote in unequivocal support. Her letter, Ulcetha kept. The rest, he burned.

The day of Osmer Trenevar's execution, Ulcetha took the Star of Cstheio to the Cairad'mazan'theileian. It was the last thing he had to do on his way out of the city.

It had been Osmer Sazamar who had suggested he might fare better at a different university.

"But where can I go?" Ulcetha said, perhaps a little despairingly.

Osmer Sazamar said, "I will write you letters of introduction to Osmer Hailenar and Osmer Padronar at the University of Choharo."

"Choharo?" said Ulcetha and thought uneasily, superstitiously, of Mara. But that was nonsense—the wreck was nothing to do with the city.

"It is an excellent university," said Osmer Sazamar, mistaking the cause of Ulcetha's unease.

"Yes, I know. I'm sorry. It just never occurred to me to *leave* Cairado."

"It is a hard thing," Osmer Sazamar said. "And it is not your only option. But if you want to achieve first-class honors… I do not think you will do it here."

Which was a gentle way of saying that Osmer Harcenar would never approve his first-class thesis, whether he wrote about shopkeepers or emperors.

"I know," Ulcetha said. "If you would write those letters, I would be very grateful."

"Of course," said Osmer Sazamar. "There has never been anything wrong with your scholarship."

That stung, just a little, but he was too conscious of what he'd been doing in his five years' banishment to protest.

He crated all of his books and left them, carefully labeled, at the central courier office, to be sent for when he had somewhere to put them. It was expensive, asking the courier office to store things, but it was worth it for his books. His other belongings, he mostly sold or gave away. Those he either could not part with or would need immediately he crated and sent ahead to the central courier office in Choharo.

In the middle of his packing, he found Sinzharo at his door again, and she again invited him down to the Cat and Carpenter for a drink. Ulcetha had too much to do and said so. She nodded, stood irresolutely for a moment, and said, "I thought it was you."

"I beg your pardon?"

"I knew Mara had a lover, but I thought it was you."

"Me?" Ulcetha tried to imagine that scenario and failed. "How…?"

"You were the only person he ever talked about."

"We were *friends.*"

"Yes, I see that now," said Sinzharo. "And I wanted to apologize."

"Oh." Ulcetha hesitated. "Well, maybe *one* drink."

It was not a wake—neither of them could afford to drink until dawn—but they split two bottles of good Flomari and talked about Mara, and Ulcetha did not get home until well past midnight. He thought a hangover would have served him right, but he went back to his packing the next day with no more than a headache, and not even a very bad one.

And then, with all of his belongings given away or sold or sent to Choharo (or waiting to be sent to Choharo—he had to stop himself almost on a daily basis from going to the courier office to check that his books were still there), the only thing remaining to do before he bought a ticket on the diligence from Cairado to Choharo was to give the Star of Cstheio back.

His third night-time trip to the Harceneise was no more eventful than the first two, and the Star of Cstheio was mercifully exactly where he had left it. He debated about taking the Neschonori book with him and finally decided that it would make him more unhappy knowing it was here, where no one would ever know about it, than having it himself, even if he couldn't explain to himself why that should be so. He also debated about the cache of stolen items from Salathgarad's shop; he could not square it with his conscience to pawn them, even though he could sorely have used the money, and he ended up taking a detour to Prince Altheva Street on his way back to Chandler Street to shove them, one by one, through the mail slot, and he could only be passionately grateful that this time no night watchman came to see what he was doing.

When he got back to his apartment, he could not settle on a safe place to put the Star of Cstheio, worrying, although he knew it was irrational, about Salathgarad bursting in and discovering it. He finally put it in the ring box he had found for it, and put the ring box under his pillow, and in that way felt it was secure enough that he was able to get some sleep.

He might, he thought, be a little frightened of Salathgarad.

In the morning, he packed a valise of pajamas and toothbrush and a clean shirt for when he got off the diligence, put the ring box in the pocket of his coat—checking once to be sure that the Star of Cstheio was still there—and set out. He stopped at the Chandler Stret zhoän for breakfast: kolveris tea and oslov and fresh peaches, and then walked down to the Athamara and found a goblin ferry.

It seemed ridiculous that this was the last time he was going to do this, and then it seemed unbearably sad, and he had to distract himself by trying to think of what he was going to say to the Cairad'athmaza before he started weeping into the river.

On the peninsula, he walked out past the remains of the First Wall and then took General Trovimar Street away from the bright shops and the municipal library into a neighborhood that had been fashionable before the Star of Cstheio was lost, but was now rundown and shabby and all in all not dissimilar to the neighborhood Ulcetha had grown up in. The Mazan'theileian of Cairado, which stood well back from the road among a grove of giant reznabeth trees, was a long, low, stone building from the reign of Prince Estora, that being the last time the mazei had had any real power in the city. It was in need of repair, which was hardly surprising, and the two novices on duty at the front door were hilariously shocked to have a visitor who wasn't a tradesman or a bill collector.

"We would like to speak to the Cairad'athmaza," Ulcetha said. "Is that possible?"

"Yes," blurted the younger novice.

The elder kicked his ankle and said, "Just a moment and we will go ask. Who should we say is calling?"

"Our name is Ulcetha Zhorvena, and we are a scholar second-class," not that they couldn't tell that from his ribbons.

"Thank you, Mer Zhorvena," said the elder novice and padded away down one of the building's long arms.

He was back very quickly and said, "The Cairad'athmaza would be very happy to speak to you. Follow us, please."

Ulcetha followed him down the hall and across a small courtyard to a circular room, cracking plaster walls and cobwebs up in the dome where it was hard to reach, bookcases—which must have been specially built—following the curve of the wall all the way around, crammed with books, rolls of parchment stacked on top. In the center of the room was a desk, clearly also specially built, since it echoed the curve of the wall, but scarred and ink-stained, with stacks of papers held down with a variety of makeshift paperweights: a sextant; a pale green glass sphere the size of Ulcetha's palm; an accounting ledger; a porcelain bowl, the glaze of which matched the glass sphere, full of paperclips; a small wooden statue of a cat. Next to the desk stood a tall, middle-aged elven man with gentle blue eyes and glasses nearly as thick as Ulcetha's.

"Mer Zhorvena?" he said. "I am Selora Athmaza. How can I help you?"

Ulcetha had tried to rehearse for this all the way out from Chandler Street, but had found himself simply unable to imagine what the right thing to say was. He held out the ring box and said, "This belongs to you."

Puzzled, Selora Athmaza took the box, opened it, and his eyes widened behind his glasses like a child's reading a wonder-tale. "Is this..."

"As far as I know," Ulcetha said carefully, "that is the Star of Cstheio. But I am no jeweler and my sources are... not impeccable."

"Where..." said Selora Athmaza. "How..."

"I would prefer not to say," Ulcetha said. He could feel the blush mounting in his face, but explaining would only make things so much worse. "I feel that the Star belongs to the Cairad'athmaz'are, so I'm returning it. That's as much as I can tell you."

"Wait wait wait!" said Selora Athmaza, rightly guessing that Ulcetha was on the point of fleeing. "You need not tell me anything you do not want to. I merely..." He looked down at the ring again.

"You will want to get a jeweler to look at it," Ulcetha said.

"Yes." Selora Athmaza looked at him, his mild blue eyes suddenly quite sharp. "And what can the Cairad'athmaz'are do for you in return?"

"What?" Ulcetha said, horrified. "Nothing! There's nothing... I mean, I'm not asking for anything."

"You're quite right. Nothing we could do could possibly be fair recompense. But you surprise me. I would have thought there would be *something*."

"There really isn't," Ulcetha said, face burning now. "And I have to go. I have a diligence to catch."

"You are leaving Cairado?" And he could see the sharp mind behind the gentle eyes putting the pieces together.

"I am."

"You were a friend of Osmer Trenevar?"

"I'm the one... I mean, ultimately, I'm the reason he was caught."

"Ah," said Selora Athmaza. "I understand."

It occurred to Ulcetha that politics in the Cairad'mazan'theileian had to be at *least* as bad as politics in the University's Department of History. He said, "So I'm just—"

"Can I write you a letter of introduction?" said Selora Athmaza. "For certainly this marks you as a friend of the mazei."

"You haven't known me for five minutes!"

"But I know a great deal about you," said Selora Athmaza. "It will only take me a moment—you notice that I am not asking you where you are going."

"Thank you. I mean, yes, thank you, if you're willing to write me a letter of introduction, I will gladly take it."

Selora Athmaza nodded. He found pen and paper and wrote swiftly, a matter of a few sentences, then folded it and handed it to Ulcetha. "Wherever you are going, go with my thanks, and the good will of the Cairad'athmaz'are."

"Thank you," said Ulcetha, putting the letter with his other letters of introduction in his inside waistcoat pocket. He and Selora Athmaza bowed to each other, and he turned and made his way out of the Cairad'mazan'theileian. As he started walking toward the Blue Boar, where the diligence for Choharo would stop, it began to rain.

About the Author

KATHERINE ADDISON'S SHORT fiction has been selected by The *Year's Best Fantasy and Horror* and *The Year's Best Science Fiction*. Her novel *The Goblin Emperor* won a Locus Award. As Sarah Monette, she is the author of the *Doctrine of Labyrinths* series and coauthor, with Elizabeth Bear, of the *Iskryne* series. She lives near Madison, Wisconsin.

@pennyvixen

@pennyvixen.bsky.social

www.katherineaddison.com